IN THE SHADOW OF OLD SMOKY

STORIES OF THE MOUNTAINS AND THEIR PEOPLE

By

C. Hodge Mathes

IN THE SHADOW OF OLD SMOKY

STORIES OF THE MOUNTAINS AND THEIR PEOPLE

By

C. Hodge Mathes

Introduced and Edited by
Charles W. Maynard

Illustrated by
Daniel Sutphin

Partner Press
SEYMOUR TENNESSEE

Foothills Land Conservancy

A royalty from <u>In the Shadow of Old Smoky Stories of the Mountains and Their People</u> will go to the Foothills Land Conservancy for the preservation of the area which C. Hodge Mathes loved and wrote about so fondly. For more information on the work of the Foothills Land Conservancy write:

Foothills Land Conservancy
352 High Street
Maryville, Tennessee 37801

ISBN 0-9630682-5-3

Photographs are from the Archives of the Great Smoky Mountains National Park and Archives and Special Collections of the Archives of Appalachia at East Tennessee State University. The front cover was photographed by Hal Hubbs. The back cover was photographed by Janice Maynard.

Illustrations are by Daniel Sutphin

We gratefully acknowledge the help of Kitty Manscill, archivist at the Great Smoky Mountains National Park, and Georgia Greer and Norma Myers of the Archives of Appalachia at East Tennessee State University.

TABLE OF CONTENTS

Introduction 7

A Saga of the Carolina Hills 13

The Linkster 20

The Draggin'est Feller 28

Simple Ike's Daughter 35

Jeff Howell's Buryin' 44

White Mule 47

The Curin'est Remedy 56

"Vengeance Is Mine!" 69

For the High Dollar 83

What Is To Be Will Be 93

Corpus Delicti 100

Willow Pattern 111

Shake Rag Shows 'Em 119

Harmony Chapel 129

Foreword to <u>Tall Tales from Old Smoky</u>, 1952 141

INTRODUCTION

Life in the Southern Mountains has changed radically in the last seventy-five years. Highways, roads, and interstates cross the mountains where footpaths and wagon roads once slowed travel to an oxen's pace. People come from all over the world to see the beauty and wonder of the mountains. The Great Smoky Mountains National Park is the most visited national park in the country, with over nine million visits each year.

The stories in this volume were written by Hodge Mathes about the mountain people he admired and enjoyed. Mathes' portrayals record an era that is long past. The photographs that accompany the stories are taken from the archives at the Great Smoky Mountains National Park and at East Tennessee State University.

All of these stories are fiction, with the exception of "A Saga of the Carolina Hills." This is not to say that the stories are not true. Hodge Mathes was dedicated to the truth. He chose to communicate truths about the mountains and their people through short stories which depicted the people both fairly and accurately. Fiction is a lens through which an era, a way of life, a truth can be brought into focus.

Charles Hodge Mathes was an educator in the highest sense of the word. He spent a great deal of time and energy throughout his life in learning. His academic credentials included: an A.B. from Washington College in 1897, a Masters from Maryville College in 1904, further work at the University of Wooster, Harvard, McGill University, and Middlebury College.

Teaching was what Hodge Mathes lived. He served as a professor at Washington College (1897-1903), Maryville College (1903-1911), East Tennessee State University (1911-1949), and Milligan College (1949-1951). In his career he taught Greek, English, Modern Languages, and Education. At one time he served East Tennessee State College (now East Tennessee State University) as dean, registrar, professor of English, professor of Education and chairman of the foreign language department.

His career in education was not without its rough spots. Ever popular with students, he sometimes ran afoul of others. Once when Dean Hodge Mathes' salary had been raised from $2,100 to $2,400, the East Tennessee Democratic leader, Thad A. Cox, complained to Governor Tom C. Rye. Cox's main objection was that Mathes was a staunch Republican.

In 1925, Hodge Mathes was nominated for the presidency of East Tennessee State Teachers College. However, Charles C. Sherrod was selected as the second president of the college. Mathes worked closely with Sherrod until both retired in 1949. Hodge Mathes did not retire voluntarily but did so only because he had reached the state mandatory retirement age of seventy. He left East Tennessee State University to teach the last two years of his life at nearby Milligan College.

Hodge Mathes believed strongly in the work he was doing at the state teachers college in Johnson City. He said that Tennessee needed "trained thinkers, professional leaders, and public servants with a broad vision, wide culture, and courageous character," and that the "training of such leaders demanded the soundest scholarship and most vigorous discipline in every field of learning." Mathes applied these words to his own life with studies in such diverse fields as archeology, architecture and history.

He wrote several books in addition to the short stories which are collected in this book. Composition and Grammar was published in 1919. With Frank Field, a fellow professor at East Tennessee State, he authored Safety in the Danger Age and Book I in the Safety Education Series. However, he did his best work in fiction about the mountains and their people.

When the Normal School and East Tennessee State Teachers College were set up in Johnson City in 1911, Hodge Mathes was the second person hired. Notes from freshmen of 1911 in the Normal School were sent to Mrs. Wynema Souder Mathes at Hodge Mathes' death. These letters of condolence express some of the character of their beloved teacher:

"Among all the teachers I had in high school, college and university days, Professor Mathes was my favorite, the one who awakened me and gave me most. He it was who made the English language a fascinating, challenging world of exquisite beauty for my exploration; who intrigued me to dare explorations in the Anglo-Saxon, the Greek, and other cultures. He imparted to me his own love of mountain climbing, and in my far travels I have remembered him particularly when struggling up some peak of the Alps or other great mountain face. He stimulated me in ways that created hungers and thirsts in my spirit for a richer life. I am deeply indebted and always will be indebted to him for his teaching and his influences upon me when I was a teen-ager."
(W. Earl Hotalen)

Archives of Appalachia, Sherrod Library
East Tennessee State University
Charles Hodge Mathes 1874 - 1951.

"Professor Mathes was one of the first teachers I met and he was assigned to teach our English Class. The first day our class met I felt I was going to enjoy this subject for Professor Mathes seemed to be so thorough and patient. This did prove to be a very interesting class and I learned something each day from his instructions. Professor Mathes had a very brilliant mind, a wonderful personality and was so kind and generous to all. I shall, indeed, remember him as a great person." (Agnes E. Dyer)

"Because he never lost his own zest for acquiring new knowledge, he was able to impart much of his own enthusiasm to his students. His search for the exact word; the finish he gave even to his informal talks; the little gesture of the head by which he emphasized a point; these all stand out in memory." (Gertrude Williams Miller)

"When we were young, with ideas shooting in all directions, and growing too fast for our clothes, we found a friend who stayed with us forty years. He smiled at us with a kindliness that steadied our nerves and made our voices more gentle, although he did seem to enjoy the bouncing vitality of that first-year class. He knew our names and natures, and how to help us through the pitfalls of adolescence. With his quick insight and obviously high cultural standards, he led us gently into a brighter world, teaching us that sympathetic understanding makes every life happier." (The First-Year Pupils in the High School, 1911, East Tennessee State Normal)

Mathes kept in touch with his students. He followed them throughout their careers. He, along with Dean Burleson, started the alumni association at East Tennessee State College in 1925. Later, in the fall of 1935, Eleanor Carlock and Mathes began publishing the <u>Alumni Quarterly</u>.

Hodge Mathes was no stranger to the mountains about which he wrote so eloquently. He was born in Maryville, Tennessee, to a Presbyterian minister and his wife on April 3, 1879. The first six years of his life, young Hodge grew up in the shadow of the Smokies while his father served a Presbyterian church in Maryville. In 1885, the family moved to Washington College in Upper East Tennessee where his father taught Greek and Latin.

When Hodge completed his first degree at Washington College he began teaching at his alma mater. In 1902 he married Wynema Souder of Indiana. They moved to Maryville in 1903 where Mathes taught Greek, Latin, and the Romance languages. The Matheses had two children, Ralph and Mildred.

The love of the mountains of East Tennessee and Western North Carolina was not just an academic or literary interest. Hodge Mathes loved to be out in the mountains, walking and climbing. In 1913, 1914, and 1915, he shared four adventurous hikes with his friend, D.R. Beeson, a Johnson City architect.

The first of these trips was a walking tour over Roan and Grandfather Mountains from August 31 to September 7. Beeson recorded their adventures in a hike journal which is illustrated with photographs taken on the trek. In 1914 they traveled to Table Rock Mountain in North Carolina from July 3 to the 6th.

Their next journey was only a few weeks later when they went by train to Kinzel Springs near Townsend, Tennessee. They walked into the Smokies from the train station to traverse the crest line of the Smokies from Spence Field to Mount Guyot. In the absence of marked trails, they often were lost. This hike roughly followed the route on which the Appalachian Trail would be blazed nearly twenty years later. They walked from August 28 to September 4. When they reached the lumber camp at Crestmont they were hungry, because they had run out of food.

On their travels, they met many people who lived and worked in the area. Beeson joked that Hodge Mathes seemed to have mutual acquaintances with nearly all the mountaineers. Mathes made friends among the people of the mountains. His stories reflect these friendships.

The fourth journey was to Mt. Mitchell in May of 1915. On this trip they met Dolph Wilson, the son of Big Tom Wilson—the hero of "A Saga of the Carolina Hills." It was on this trip that they heard the tale that Mathes recorded in that story.

Hodge Mathes made many other hiking trips into the mountains. The walks with Beeson were well documented with text and pictures. Mathes drew on these walking experiences as he wrote his own fictional accounts of life in the mountains. His familiarity with the geography of the region is evident from his writings. Often the actual names of places and geographical points were fictionalized. However, those that are familiar with the terrain of East Tennessee and Western North Carolina are never lost in Hodge Mathes' stories.

In addition to his love of the mountains, Hodge Mathes had a love of languages. His ear for languages and dialects is well recorded in his stories. He was a "linkster" who could listen to and reproduce everyday talk. This was a day before tape recorders. His memory for languages must have been excellent. The fact that he was proficient in several languages (Greek, Latin, German, French, Italian, and Russian) is evidence enough.

The stories that Mathes wrote show his own use of English. His command of the language is beautiful. He records the dialect of the mountain people with accuracy and respect. Reading the mountain dialect can be difficult. Sometimes it is best to read it aloud so that the sound of the words can be heard. Mathes enjoyed the mountain speech because it sometimes preserved Elizabethan English.

The stories in this volume were first published in magazines and journals from 1923 to 1940. After his death in 1951, Mathes' wife, Wynema, collected some of his stories in a volume that she entitled <u>Tall Tales From Old Smoky</u>. Most of the stories were not exactly tall tales, but the book did well enough in the area. Reprints of the original were published in 1975 and 1992. Most of the stories in this present volume appeared in <u>Tall Tales From Old Smoky</u>.

Several interesting threads run throughout the tapestry of Mathes' stories. The prime movers in eight of the fourteen stories are women or girls. Mountain women were often seen as silent partners to their husbands. However, Mathes brings them to the forefront in many of his stories.

With his background of being raised in a Presbyterian manse, it is no wonder that churches and preachers play central roles in many stories. This also reflects the fact that next to the family, the church was the primary social institution in mountain communities. The pastor was a central figure and often looked to for wise advice.

Mathes' picture of the mountain preacher wasn't always complimentary. In several stories the preacher was the one who stood against change from the outside world. This characterization only points up the church's role as guardian of the common good. Usually change was viewed with a suspicious eye.

Archives of Appalachia, Sherrod Library
East Tennessee State University

D.R. Beeson, Sr., Papers

Hodge Mathes beside a large tree on the May 1915 hike to Mt. Mitchell.

A third theme is that of education. Schools and school teachers play a part in five of the fourteen stories. Mathes' own vocation as a teacher obviously influenced this interest. However, Mathes did not always treat the teachers kindly. In "Simple Ike's Daughter" he pokes at his own profession while telling the story of a mountain girl's own genius.

Doctors and mountain medicine are a fourth topic that Mathes enjoyed addressing in his stories. Mountain medicine was one of the traditions that intrigued Hodge Mathes. The curing that took place with the lack of medical science was interesting. "The Curin'est Remedy" points to the fact that perhaps there is something to both sides of the coin. Science and folk medicine offered varied solutions to the same illnesses with varied results.

In general, Hodge Mathes simply loved the people of the mountains. Whenever he listened to the mountain talk of his highland neighbors it was with a sympathetic ear. His stories reflect the sheer joy of this man who reveled in the mountains and their people.

For those who grew up in another era, these stories will be pleasant reminders of that day. To others who never knew the time and place, these tales will dispel the darkness that time has brought. These stories are again presented so that all might see what life once was in the shadow of Old Smoky.

Charles W. Maynard
March, 1994

A SAGA OF THE CAROLINA HILLS

Nearly every schoolboy knows to-day that the highest mountain in the eastern part of the United States is Mount Mitchell, in North Carolina. A much smaller number, with a head for remembering figures, might possibly recall the altitude of that mountain—6,711 feet above the sea, though surprisingly few school geographies seem to record either of these two facts. Far smaller still, I dare say, is the number of either children or grown-ups who have ever heard the story of how this crowning peak of eastern North America came to bear the name of Mitchell.

The chief actors in that story are two men: one a noted scholar and scientist, the other a gigantic hillsman, a mighty hunter of the bear and deer that for ages have roamed the vastnesses of the great Appalachian hinterland. It was from the lips of a son of this stalwart old hunter that I have heard, not once but often, many of the details of this true story that have never found their way into print. It has also been my good fortune to know at first hand and intimately the indescribably wild and remote region that furnishes the setting for the tale.

That region, to be sure, has now been discovered by the tourist, and a few of its outstanding points of interest may to-day be reached by motor. On my earliest visits, nearly a score of years ago, the only way to see Mount Mitchell or any of the vast wonderland of the Black Mountains was to go afoot, picking one's way through the eternal twilight of virgin forest along ancient trails that buffaloes, bears, and Indians had made long before a white man had ever glimpsed the Blue Ridge.

To begin the story properly we must go back nearly a decade before the Civil War. To most Americans at that time the great mountain masses of Tennessee and the Carolinas were a veritable *terra incognita*, sparsely populated by straggling descendants of the pioneers of the first transmontane migration, and inaccessible save by a few steep and dangerous oxcart roads that sooner or later petered out among the highest hills into steeper and more dangerous bridle paths or game trails.

No official surveys of the Southern Appalachians had been undertaken by the government, and the altitude of the remote peaks of the Blue Ridge, the Unakas, and Great Smoky was unknown. Conflicting estimates, partly guess-work, partly based upon inaccurate private surveys and colored by local pride, were to be found in the fragmentary accounts that occasionally appeared in print.

A certain peak in Great Smoky, now known as Clingmans Dome (altitude 6,619 feet), was generally believed to be the highest point in the Appalachian system, and its height was often declared to be upward of 8,000 feet. Most New Englanders, on the other hand, stoutly maintained that Mount Washington in the White Mountains was the loftiest peak in the Eastern States.

About 1856 a committee in Congress was considering a request presented by certain citizens of North Carolina that the "Dome" of the Black Mountains, having been definitely ascertained to be the highest peak in the State, should be officially named Clingman's Peak, in honor of Hon. Thomas L. Clingman, of Buncombe County, who had served in the House of Commons and the Senate of the State and had been elected to Congress for a number of terms.

Before action had been taken upon this request the friends of Rev. Elisha Mitchell, professor of chemistry and geology in the State University at Chapel Hill, began to press the prior claims of this eminent and widely beloved scientist to receive the honor that was about to be bestowed upon the favorite political son.

Professor Mitchell was now about sixty-four years of age and had spent nearly forty years as an instructor in the University of his adopted State. A modest, retiring New England clergyman and geologist and mineralogist of note, he had endeared himself to all classes in the State. For years he had served as State surveyor and had spent many summers in the mountain sections on scientific explorations of various sorts.

The pupils, colleagues, and neighbors of Professor Mitchell now urged him, rather against his personal inclinations, to take steps to prove his claims as the real "discoverer" of the Black Dome, and a petition was prepared asking that the peak be given the name of Mitchell.

Toward the end of June, 1857, Professor Mitchell set out with a small party of friends to revisit the mountain which, twenty years before, he had first explored and had declared to be the highest peak in the system. It was his plan to look up some of the native guides and helpers who had accompanied him on that survey and secure their sworn statements to be filed with other documentary proofs with the Congressional committee.

It was a long and toilsome journey from Asheville to the balsam-crowned summit of the Dome, where he had years ago set a rough stone marker to indicate what he had calculated to be the highest point of land east of the Rockies. Having reached the top, however, Mitchell determined to dismiss his companions and to continue his journey, afoot and alone, down into the deep valley on the Yancey side of the great ridge, where he wished to secure an affidavit from an old trapper and guide by the name of Green. He knew he could count on the help and the hospitality of the loyal mountaineers who had come to know and love the "Perfesser" in years gone by.

That parting with his friends at the top of the Black Dome was the last time Elisha Mitchell was ever seen alive. When he had not returned on the third day his family became alarmed. Next day a small searching party set out to find him. It was soon learned that he had never reached the home of his old guide, and none of the mountain folk had seen or heard of him.

A general alarm was now given, and a large party, headed by the popular statesman, Zebulon Baird Vance, began a day-and-night manhunt, combing one after another of the interminable ridges and ravines with dogs and lanterns and keeping in touch with each other by prearranged gunshot signals. Several days passed, however, without a single trace of the lost man. The whole State was aroused, from the cities of the Coastal Plain to the scattered settlements of the western mountains.

On the tenth or eleventh day the distressing news had penetrated to a sequestered cove on the farther side of the Blacks. Here a small party was organized by one of the most romantic characters that ever lived in the Carolina hills, "Big Tom" Wilson, gigantic of frame, a stranger to fear, and familiar with every mile of the dark wilderness of the Black Mountains. Big Tom possessed in a remarkable degree that almost uncanny power that few save the Indians have ever acquired, of reading the "signs" of man or beast in the woods.

The veteran hunter led his party of seasoned mountain men to the top of the Dome and securing from the watchers there the meager details of Mitchell's last conversation with his Asheville friends, took up the search by a plan all his own.

Learning that the Professor had declared his intention of following the old "Beech Nursery" trail to the foot of the mountain, Big Tom and his party set out in single file, the sinewy giant in the lead. He had gone scarcely half a mile when his practiced eye caught something significant that all the other parties had missed.

Archives of Appalachia, Sherrod Library　　　　　　　　　　D.R. Beeson, Sr., Papers
East Tennessee State University

Hodge Mathes with Niagra Falls Riddle, the granddaughter of Big Tom Wilson, at Big Tom's old home place in 1914.

"Look, boys!" he exclaimed. "Right here's whar the ol' man missed the trail! Instid of bearin' on to the left, like he ought, he turned off down t'wards the Piny Ridge. An' right that minute he was lost, an' *bad* lost!"

Sure enough, as they pressed on down the right-hand trail, which was probably only a bear path, here and there appeared the faint but still recognizable tracks of a man, headed toward the desolate waste under the frowning tops of the twin peaks known as the "Black Brothers."

"He couldn't have been makin' no time in here, boys," Big Tom declared half an hour later as the going grew worse and more dangerous. "See how he's had to tromp down the bresh an' scrouge through the laurel! An' here's a piece tore out of his coat!"

Two miles or more they pushed on—slow, wearisome miles even for the sturdy mountaineers. For the aged scientist, long unpracticed in such tramping, it must have been a grilling experience.

"Here's whar dark overtuck him," the guide announced after another mile had been covered. "Look whar he twisted him a pine knot out o' this ol' log an' made him a torch! Here's a coal that drapped when he crossed this rock!"

Two more miles, through tangled briars, over jagged ledges, and down the boulder-strewn bed of a little creek.

"'Course by this time he knowed he was lost," the leader commented, "but he figgered that this here creek would take him to the Cane River, which naturally hit would, only hit's a turrible way to git thar!"

A few hundred yards more and the roar grew louder. They were on the very top of the ledge.

"Look, boys!" Big Tom sang out. "He was tryin' to git around on the right of this place in the nighttime! See, he grabbed holt of this little saplin' an' his foot slipped on this slick rock. The saplin' broke off in his hand! Boys, that pore ol' man has fell right over them falls! We'll find him down thar as shore as the world!"

Clambering down over the rocks and through the undergrowth, the party at last reached the foot of the cliff, over which tumbled a foaming cascade approximately twenty feet high. At its foot was a dark, deep, jug-shaped pool of swirling foam ten or twelve feet across. Even the strongest swimmer could not have kept afloat in that mad little whirlpool.

At first they could see nothing in the churning water, but finally Big Tom made out a dark object underneath the surface lying across a sunken birch log that had long ago fallen into the pool. And in the gloom of that sunless gorge they lifted the body of Elisha Mitchell from its watery tomb.

Sadly and with prodigious labor they bore their burden back up the long miles and delivered it to the friends waiting at the top. Big Tom and the other mountaineers urged that it be laid to rest there on the spot that his travels and explorations had made memorable, but other counsels prevailed, and the body was carried back to Asheville and buried in the Presbyterian cemetery.

Years afterwards, however, when government surveys had confirmed Mitchell's calculations and the Black Dome, officially and finally named in his honor, had become one of the chief points of scenic and historic interest in the State, the bones were exhumed and carried back to be deposited in a rocky grave at the very summit of the peak.

A modest shaft of hollow bronze bearing a simple inscription was erected by relatives and friends at the grave, but the fierce storms that sweep the summit finally wrecked it. Then a wooden observation tower, built by the State Park Commission, took its place. This was later replaced by a steel tower, but it also fell before the fury of the winds. Very recently a beautiful and massive tower of stone, the gift of a public-spirited citizen of the State, has been reared on the site of the grave. Its top, rising above the low timber, affords one of the most impressive panoramas to be found on the American continent.

Of late Mount Mitchell has come into its own as a goal for the throngs of those who go "seeing America first." It is one of the show places of the South. Two

Archives of Appalachia, Sherrod Library
East Tennessee State University

D.R. Beeson, Sr., Papers

Dolph Wilson pointing to Mitchell Falls where his father, Big Tom, found the body of Rev. Elijah Mitchell. The photograph was made on the hike D.R. Beeson and Hodge Mathes made in August 1914.

excellent motor roads have been built to the top, and thousands of tourists make the ascent each season.

Frankly, though, this mountaineering *de luxe* does not give much of a thrill to those of us who used to camp under the big "rock-house" just below the top, or in the old log cabin that later stood there. Dearer to us were those never-to-be-forgotten nights under the stars, where the cool wind in the balsams and the occasional scream of a wild cat or a mountain owl gave us a weird sense of solitariness, knowing we were the only human beings in the vast loneliness of the Black Mountains.

Big Tom Wilson lived more that fifty years after what he always called his greatest adventure, the finding of Mitchell's body. He was the greatest hunter and trapper in all the mountain settlements. One hundred and fourteen black bears fell to his rifle, a record as yet unsurpassed, as far as I have authentic information, in the Southern Appalachians.

Honest to the core, king of heart, keenly intelligent although unlettered, devoutly religious, and thrifty as only a canny Scotch-Irish hillsman knows how to be, he left a goodly estate of mountain lands, a worthy family of sons and daughters, and a name that is yet honored in his native hills. In the sequestered world in which he lived his eighty-five years he reigned as one of nature's own princes. Quite fittingly the beautiful valley where his cabin home stood and still stands is marked on the topographic maps of the Geological Survey as "Big Tom Wilson's."

His sons and his sons' sons have preserved the estate and cherished the traditions of their doughty progenitor. It was one of these sons, Dolph Wilson, himself now nearing seventy, who gave me much of the story I have recorded here. With him I have tramped the obscure trail over which his father piloted the searchers for Mitchell's body. Only with such a guide could one ever hope to find the desolate "Mitchell's Falls," a spot that few visitors have ever seen.

Dolph is himself a veteran nimrod and has killed a total of a hundred and eleven bears. It is characteristic of the man that he has now quit the chase for good, not because of his age but in order that his father's famous record shall continue unbroken in the traditions of the bear country. Dolph has prospered far beyond the average of mountain folk and is reputed wealthy in the hills. He is a local magistrate and his "court" is wholesomely feared by the petty lawbreaker. Fortunate is the party of tourists who can nowadays have Dolph Wilson as a guide. He is a bush man, for despite his sixty-eight years he patrols almost daily an extensive boundary that he has leased as a game preserve to a hunting and fishing camp in Asheville, and he can still walk the legs off a tenderfoot.

Dolph Wilson represents the finest traditions of the sturdy pioneers. He loves to sit on his porch in the starlight and tell of the early days—the old rifles, the old trails, the old customs. But he looks the modern world level in the face with an eye as cool as that which used to gaze down the sights of his trusty Winchester at a wounded and charging bear.

THE LINKSTER

The door of my classroom opened softly, and the assistant janitor entered apologetically.

"Pardon me, professor. There are two women in the corridor below who wish to speak to you. They look like mountain women and wouldn't state their business to me. I told them you were probably busy."

"No, Williams, I'm not teaching at this hour," I replied. "Show them upstairs if you will."

The clatter of heavy shoes sent an unwonted echo through the quiet hallway. In a moment two slatternly women stood hesitant at the threshold of the room.

"Mister," the older and bolder inquired, "air you a linkster?"

"Beg pardon, madam, am I a *what*?" I asked, a bit dazed at the unusual query.

"Air you a linkster?" the woman repeated. "We've jist come from Lawyer Taylor's office down yander in town, an' he 'lowed jedgmatically ye was."

"Well, I've been called a good many things, and if my friend Judge Taylor says I'm this particular thing, he's probably right. But I think you'll have to tell me just what a linkster is or what he does."

"Why, Mister, a linkster's a feller that can read writin' er understand talkin' in a furrin tongue—say like Injun er Dutch er somethin' thataway."

I began to see the light. "Linkster" —why, of course, "lingister" —a forgotten Appalachian word I seemed to have known somewhere before. Not strange that in a land where a foreigner is as rare as the dodo the word for "interpreter" should have faded from most men's memory.

"Why, I'm afraid I'm not the kind of one you wish," I replied. "I know nothing of any Indian tongues and very little of Dutch, though I do know some foreign languages and teach two of them in this college. But why do you ask?"

"Why, Mister, we've got all bumfuzzled about a letter that come in the mail t'other day. Hit's writ in some kind of writin' that nobody in Dry Cove can't read hit. Squar Gaby he 'lowed hit was Dutch er Latting maybe, so I brung hit to town an' showed hit to Lawyer Taylor an' he 'lowed you could interpetate hit."

"Possibly I might," I said, "Have you the letter with you?"

"Yes, sir, we fotch hit," the older woman continued. "Virgie, give hit to the man."

The younger woman, a girl of probably twenty years, drew a tinted square envelope from a pocket in her long, loose, incredibly old-fashioned coat. The flat voice of the old woman went on.

"We was fearful hit mought be about my boy. He's in the war—somers on yan side. His name's John Hilton, an' this here's his wife, Virgie Hilton."

"Oh, I begin to understand now," I answered, taking the letter. "This is written in French, and I can read it easily enough. Shall I translate it for you?"

"Yes, sir, I reckon that's what you call hit. We want to know who hit's from an' what hit says."

"Well, come in and sit down and I will read it to you. Then if you wish, I will have a stenographer make a copy in English so that you can read for yourselves."

"They wouldn't be no needcessity of that Mister. Can't nary one of us read no kind of writin' ner printin', but we can recollec' the main idy of it if you'll read it off, like."

The letter, as a glance revealed, was from a girl in a tiny village of northern France. It was addressed to the father and mother of John Hilton who, at the time of writing, was billeted in the home of the French girl's parents. The note had been laboriously but crudely penned and there were numerous errors of composition, but it was typically and eloquently "Frenchy." I glanced hastily through its contents before I began to translate it aloud.

Instantly I saw the situation. Either the simple-minded peasant girl had been dazzled by the glamour of a stalwart American doughboy, or the simple-minded doughboy had fallen easy prey to the wiles of the village vampire. The girl's letter gave it all away. The boy was her lover. He had promised to marry her and bring her to America. To surprise him she was secretly writing this message to his parents after beguiling him to give her their names and address.

She loved dear Jean very, very much and would try very, very hard to be a good *belle-fille* to her dear *beau-père* and dear *belle-mère* in America. She was

Courtesy of the Great Smoky Mountains National Park

Hauling produce to market with an ox and wooden wagon.

praying the Holy Mother every day that he might be kept from harm in the terrible war, and the old priest in the village was praying, too. She was sending a thousand kisses and most tender caresses to the dear parents of Jean, and was, with sincere affection, their humble and most dutiful daughter, Héloïse Michaud.

I had read the letter through rapidly, partly in order that if it told of any mishap befallen the son and husband at the front, I might soften somewhat the blow of evil tidings for the mother and wife; but this was something I wasn't prepared for. Apparently my plain business as a "linkster" was simply to translate the message as it stood. It was no affair of mine, anyhow. I had merely been called in to render a slight favor to total strangers whom I should probably never see again.

So I reasoned, and turned in my swivel-chair to read; but a second glance at the young wife changed my decision in a twinkling. The older woman's face wore that stoical, unreadable expression that the years bring to the hardy mothers of mountain men.

But the girl-wife's large hazel eyes were fixed on me with a wondering, hoping, agonizing appeal that strangely belied the outward calm she maintained. Despite the formless drapery of the heavy coat she wore this warm autumn morning, it was apparent that her great hour was but a matter of a few weeks—perhaps a few days. And I held in my hand a letter from the far-away unknown somewhere, whither they had sent her man and the father of her babe. News of him was now to break the silence of the anxious months since that last blissful week he had been given to spend at home.

And that is why I, a respectable professor of modern languages in a staid old college—I, a deacon in the Presbyterian church, deliberately made that French letter read, as nearly as I can now recall, like this:

Dear Friends in America:
      This is to give you news of your dear son John Hilton, who for some weeks has been stationed in this village preparatory to being transferred to the front lines. He wishes me to tell you that he is well and happy and is being as well cared for as possible in our little home. He speaks of you every day, especially of his father and mother and his dear young wife. I am praying the Holy Mother each day that he may be kept from harm in the terrible war. He says that if you can find some one to write he can have the letter read by a comrade or by the old priest in the village. With sincere affection from your unknown friends in France, I am

                Affectionately yours,
                HÉLOÏSE MICHAUD

The contents of the letter as thus rendered were eminently satisfactory to the listeners. Even the mother's expressionless countenance lighted with a smile that exposed the two ugly yellow snags in her shrunken mouth and threw into startling contrast the singularly perfect ivory teeth of the girl. The inexpressible relief and happiness shining in every line of the young wife's radiant face made me brazenly indifferent as to the probable attitude of the Recording Angel toward my well-intentioned duplicity.

"She shore writes like a good gal, don't she, Virgie?" the mother ejaculated when I had finished.

"Yes, an' awful religious-like, too. She talks plumb purty!"

"Well, Mister—er—Perfesser, I reckon I ort to say—we're much obleeged to ye fer readin' hit to us. We're pore folks an' hain't got nothin' much, but if ye ever git out in them mountings yander we'd be real proud fer ye to drap in. We'll be gittin' along now." And with their gratitude voiced thus eloquently in the crude phrases of bygone days, they stalked out of the room.

I watched them as they crossed the campus, their rustic dress and carriage made the more conspicuous as they passed a group of college girls at the gate. But as in fancy I followed their awkward footsteps out of the little city and along the dusty miles to where the undulating azure of the Cherokee range softened into the southern skyline, I couldn't help feeling a bit prouder of my proficiency in the Romance Languages than I'd every been before!

And yet there was one disconcerting fly in the ointment of my complacency. That was the fear that, in the canny, suspicious way our mountain folk have in their dealings with strangers, they should decide to corroborate my rendering of the strange letter by seeking the aid of another "linkster." I blamed myself for not having written my "translation" and substituted it for the original, keeping the latter in my possession.

The incident of the French letter had been all but forgotten in the busy routine of the spring semester's work, when one day at the luncheon hour I was taking a few moments' exercise by strolling along the maple-lined walks in the college yard. My attention was drawn to a canvas-covered farm wagon—a mountain edition of the prairie schooner—passing in the street. Supposing it to be one of the innumerable apple wagons from the near-by mountains and thinking to purchase a choice Virginia Beauty or Gilliflower for a dessert, I passed through the gate and accosted the driver, a gaunt graybeard in homespun.

"No, Mister, I never fotch nary apple this trip," he replied to my inquiry. "I jist come to town to do some tradin' an' git news from the war."

"You have a son overseas?" I asked, divining it from something in the old man's tone.

"I *did* have, Mister," he said quietly. "But Lawyer Taylor give me this here paper this mornin' an' says my boy's named among the killed. Here's the paper—the Jedge he put a mark ferinst the name." And he handed me the folded paper.

I saw the name Judge Taylor had checked: "John Hilton, Dry Cove, Tennessee." Then I remembered. "Oh! Then it was your wife and daughter-in-law who brought me the letter from the young French woman some months ago."

"Yes, sir, an' I reckon you're the linkster they talked about so much. They was shore proud the way ye holp 'em!"

"Well, my dear sir, I am sorry indeed to know of your great loss," I said, extending my hand.

"Much obleeged, Perfesser," the old man answered with dry eyes but with a choke in his voice. "Hit's a hard thing, sir, to raise a boy an' then him be tuck away off to some furrin country an' killed when nuther you ner him didn't have nary thing to do with the trouble, ner even know rightly what hit was all about. But, sir, the wust of hit fer me is in goin' home an' tellin' the ol' woman an' the boy's woman. She' a-nussin' a babe now, that's named fer hit's daddy. Hit's a sorry time, sir!"

"It is indeed, my friend, and I shall ask you to express to your wife and your son's wife my sympathy in this great sorrow that falls so heavily upon mothers and wives in these troubled times."

"That's a good kind word, Mister, an hit'll do the women-folks a heap o' good. They keep a-tellin' about ye an' sayin' how clever ye was to 'em."

The canvas-covered wagon rumbled on. The dry eyes of the old man were turned toward the blue hills where that night two mothers should pour down their little rivulet of tears to swell the mighty flood of the world's grief. With a pang there came to me again the thought of the telltale letter. The old mother of a fallen soldier and the young mother of a fatherless babe would weep that night, but their tears would be soft and cleansing, leaving no scars. Any day, though, a chance stranger might break the fragile phial I had sealed with kindly deception, and its acrid poison would flow into the freshly opened wounds to scald and sear past all healing.

Many months passed; there were signs of spring again. On a crisp Saturday morning I had donned tramping togs, slung knapsack and camera across my shoulders, and fared forth for a day in the hills. In three hours I was in the shadows of the Cherokee. The state highway from the city had long since given place to a fairly good "dirt road," and this in turn had narrowed and roughened into a rocky wagon way that followed along, across, and through a tumbling stream between steep wooded ridges. Here and there the mountain walls parted far enough to frame in a bit of meadow with a cabin and a stable nestling against the foot of the ridge. Occasional flashes of azalea startled the eye from the mountain-sides. Furry-looking scrub cattle huddled about weathered haystacks.

Then the road led upward more sharply, with innumerable windings, until it crossed the top of the main ridge in a sunny gap. Here by a tiny spring I stopped for an early lunch. Behind and below me the valley lay in the hazy sunlight. Short stretches of the roadway I had followed showed as yellow streaks against the green forest background.

In the distance I descried a white object moving almost imperceptibly along one of these yellow streaks. I soon made it out as a mountaineer's white-topped wagon, coming up toward the gap. By the time I had eaten my sandwiches and drunk my coffee the rumble of wheels on the rocks could be heard. I sat and waited until the wagon pulled up to the spring.

It took me some moments to make sure I had seen the white-haired teamster before, but he recognized me instantly. Mountaineers never forget a stranger. He greeted me in the old emotionless tone I now recalled distinctly. I had advanced to the wagon and was about to make some jocular remark about his apparently heavy load, when a shock of realization came to me. Protruding from the open end-gate of the short wagon, beneath the canvas top, was the end of a long box draped with an American flag.

"Oh, I see," I gasped. "Your son, back from France!"

"Yes, Mister. I'm a-buryin' him tomorrer."

I grasped the old man's hand and he gripped mine in a way that meant understanding.

"How much farther do you go?" I asked.

"Hit's jist a little ways down around the next p'int. Won't ye go home with me? The ol' woman an' the gal would be proud to see ye, sir."

Without a word I climbed up and sat beside him. As we neared the journey's end I could see that my aged companion was becoming ill at ease; his stolid manner grew less confident. It was plain that he dreaded the moment of arrival.

"Ye know how women-folks is, sir," he said as if to fortify me as well as himself against the trying scene he anticipated. "They'll be a right smart of a crowd thar, I reckon. The ol' woman's nephew, a young feller that's 'tendin' college over at Maryville, is thar. He's a smart lad an' they say he gits his sheepskin nex' spring."

The women met us at the gate with no outcry or demonstration, to the old man's relief. They wiped a few tears away with the corners of their aprons as the neighbor men removed the casket from the box, laid the flag upon it, and carried it into the house. Both women greeted me cordially, but betrayed not the least surprise at my unexpected presence. A score of neighbors sat quietly within, on chairs, benches or beds. The black metallic casket was placed upon two chairs in the center of the room. There was no service, no prayer, no preacher. The family and friends had come to sit awhile with the dead.

The young kinsman from the college, a trim-looking youth, sat near the head of the bier. Virgie's baby, little John, struggled down from his mother's lap and toddled on sturdy but uncertain legs about the room. The grandmother quietly dominated the little group, welcoming newcomers, closing doors, piling fresh logs on the open fire. When all were seated she went to the old "press" in the corner of the room, opened its calico-curtained door, and drew from a hidden recess a sadly worn tinted envelope.

"Frien's an' neighbors," she began in a voice that was calm and steady, "some of you-uns has heard about the nice letter we got from the Frinch lady whilst John was on yan side. The Perfesser that's with us today read hit to me an' Virgie an' hit was as purty talkin' as ever I heard. We've got my sister's boy here from college, which he's l'arnt to read them furrin tongues right offen the book, an' I'm goin' to ax him to taken an' read this letter to you-uns. Hit makes us proud of the way John helt hisself up amongst the best of 'em when he got over yander."

A cold sweat broke out on my forehead and a sickening horror seized me. My worst fears had been realized and the tragic undeceiving was to come on this day of days, the home-coming of the hero son, now to be turned into a day of confusion and humiliation. I tried to think of something—anything—to prevent the awful thing that was going to happen. I conceived a wild, impossible plan to interrupt, to make some excuse to call the college boy aside, make a hurried explanation, and coach him for the translation. But it was too late.

The grandmother started to cross the room to place the letter in the young man's hands. Little John clung to her skirts and whimpered to be taken up. A new thought came to her.

"Here, honey," she said gently, "you take this here letter over yander an' give hit to your Cousin Davy. That's Granny's leetle man, bless his heart!"

The guests smiled soberly as the baby, clutching the letter in his hand, began his wobbly journey across the room. In his childish mind he realized that he had an important mission to perform, but he wasn't exactly sure what was expected of him. Midway of his course he stopped, turned back and looked at his grandmother, who shook her gray head in encouragement. Then a light of understanding shone in his baby eyes. He took two quick steps forward and tossed the letter upon the blazing logs in the great stone fireplace!

With a cry of dismay the grandmother started toward the fire, but by the time her stiff joints could respond and her rheumatic hands could seize the tongs, there was left only the scorched corner of the last page. It bore the French girl's name—Héloïse Michaud.

I was on my feet in an instant. My brain was working now—working as if by inspiration.

"My dear friends," I said, "you are all distressed, of course, over what has just happened to the letter. Fortunately I can recall practically every word of it, and I am going to write it all again in French, just as I read it to my two friends more than a year ago. I know they will wish to keep it, and that this little boy, when he grows to manhood, will treasure it as a memorial of his brave young father who gave his life for a great cause."

A vision of the grateful, tear-shiny faces of an old woman and a young widow went with me down the rough homeward road that afternoon. I don't know what the Recording Angel put down in the Big Books, but I do know I was a very unrepentant and very happy linkster!

THE DRAGGIN'EST FELLER

He was a new man, or he would have known better. No old-timer on the woods gang would have been rash enough to expose himself to the deadly repartee of Draggin' Ellick, teamster ordinary and humorist extraordinary, in the employ of the Clear Prong Lumber Company. The newcomer had been taken on that morning by Jim Roberts, the woods boss, and put to work on the skidder crew. He was a seasoned-looking roughneck in new overalls and with new rawhide laces in his stout logger's boots. He handled ax and peavey with a skill that excited the admiration of the foreman and the envy of the crew.

When the noon whistle blew the skidder boys hustled down to the mess shack of Camp Six, where the loggers and loaders of the Roberts outfit had already gone through the washing-up process and were seated about the shack awaiting the cook's artistic rendition of a popular air on the brass dinner bell.

Last of all came Ellick Hendrix. As usual, he had taken time to rub down and feed his big Clydesdales before coming to the shack for his own feed. He was a big, loosely constructed mountaineer, saved from corpulence only by living perforce the rigorous life of a woods husky. His full-fed cheeks shone rosily above a week's growth of reddish stubble mixed with streaks of incipient gray. He crossed the foot-log over the branch and greeted the crowd with stentorian jollity.

"Howdy, ever'body! Hit's the good ol' time o' day ag'in!"

Then he caught sight of the stranger seated on an inverted tub and leaning against the wall of the shack, his hat on the ground beside him.

"Howdy, stranger!" Ellick shouted at the top of his voice. "How does yer copporosity 'pear to segashiate?"

The effort at a pleasantry was older than the oldest man on the works—older than everything in sight except the ancient hills—but not too old to raise a roar of laughter, supposed at the new man's expense. All joined in the laugh save the stranger himself. He looked a bit sheepish, but when the last haw-haw had died away, responded cheerfully:

"All right, mister, an' how d'ye come on?"

Ellick Hendrix had not come by sobriquet of "Draggin' Ellick" by accident. And by the way, lest the plainsman reader find no light from his flatwoods dictionary upon this word "draggin'," he is hereby apprised that in Appalachia, where we are content to keep the English in the form that was good enough for Ben Johnson, Shakespeare, and Bunyan, "drag" still means, on occasion, to embarrass or silence by swift and telling repartee.

It mattered not to Ellick or his audience that his jokes were hoary with age and his most effective sallies often utterly pointless. They were delivered with such dispatch and gusto, and followed by such explosions and reverberations of his own laughter that they carried the crowd by storm. The luckless victim could only cower in his shell-hole until the barrage was lifted. It was unfortunate, therefore, that the stranger in camp should have drawn the enemy's fire by shooting off his innocent little popgun, "How d'ye come on?"

"Why, pardner, I come on my *feet*! How did ye reckon I come? Haw! Haw!" And the gang screamed their mirth just as though they had not heard the same old mountain gag a hundred times before.

The new man looked a little dazed, but said nothing until the merriment had subsided again, when he smilingly observed: "Well, ye 'low ye drug me that time, don't ye, mister?"

Instantly the answer flashed. "Ye look like the buzzards had drug *you* till ye rubbed all the *ha'r* offen the back o' yer head!" This had obvious reference to the bald spot the stranger exposed when he removed his hat. In the roar that followed this second hit, Ole Pete, the cook, joined, and his fat sides shook in cadence with the rhythmic dinner-bell solo.

At the table the new hand, whose time card bore the name Dave Howell, found himself seated opposite Draggin' Ellick, who, flushed with two fresh triumphs of his wit, was still thirsty for blood. Howell was too busy with knife and fork—mostly knife—to take much part in the boisterous meal-time banter, but whenever he did venture even the most common-place remark it was greeted with a salvo from the bristling fort across the table. To be sure, the shots went wild, aimed at nothing and hitting nothing, but Ellick's contagious haw-haws never failed to set the company in a roar.

Howell, having been for three days out of a job, ate with an appetite that attracted attention even in a logging camp, and when all the rest were tilting back their chairs and exploring their pockets for goose-quill toothpicks, he was just entering the pie phase of the dietetic cycle. This circumstance offered Draggin' Ellick the pretext for a parting shot.

"Take yer time, pardner," he counseled as he rose to leave. "I 'low yer daddy eat powerful fast an' yer mammy eat a long time, an' ye 'pearently tuck atter both of 'em!"

If Dave Howell, though, was seriously embarrassed by his warm reception at the hands of the camp humorist, he kept the fact to himself. Already established in the good graces of the boss by his deftness in handling logs, he soon won the hearts of the men by an equal deftness in spinning yarns. Some of his first efforts as a raconteur were taken seriously, as they were apparently meant to be, but it was soon a matter of common knowledge and local pride that Camp Six was honored by the presence of a fancy liar of no ordinary gifts.

If there is any rhetorical accomplishment the woodsman holds in equal esteem with brilliant repartee, it is artistic lying. Crude everyday fibbing he righteously scorns as contemptible and unscriptural, but for the veritable whopper that spurns the petty bounds of facts and figures in the higher interests of spellbinding idealism, he knows no feeling but admiration.

Dave Howell was that kind of liar, a Munchausen of the lumber camps, who wore his title of "Lyin' Dave" with modest but honorable pride. Within a week he had become a formidable rival of Draggin' Ellick as the chief intellectual ornament of Camp Six. Of evenings in the bunk-house the favorite program would open with the strains of "Sourwood Mountain" or "Arkansas Traveler" from Fletch McCurry's banjo, or perchance a clog dance by Pete Gates, whose immense scow-bottom feet flopped and shuffled on the boards like an earthquake set to music. Then over in the corner Dave Howell would begin: "When I were a-filin' saws fer the Ca'liny Spruce Comp'ny over on the Yancey side of the Black Mountings, there were a old-like feller come thar by the name of—"

"Stop that racket, you feller!" someone would call out. "Lyin' Dave's fixin' to tell another'n!" And Dave would have the floor, with one of his homely romances, whether of the tallest hemlock, the biggest band-mill, the pullin'est team of hosses, the cussin'est boss, or the luckiest hand of cards that ever was on land or sea.

Courtesy of the Great Smoky Mountains National Park Tipton Collection

A log skid at Sugarlands used by the Little River Lumber Company.

Seldom, though, did the evening's entertainment end without a sword-clash between Howell and Draggin' Ellick. The gang expected it, and Ellick always strove to please. For him, indeed, it was a never-failing triumph, and cheaply won at that.

Occasionally, though, Howell would put up at least a semblance of counter-offensive. Being nobody's fool in particular, he would sometimes deliver a neat retort that on its merits would have put the laugh squarely upon his tormentor; but Dave's manner was too mild and his humor too subtle for an audience schooled in the knock-down-and-drag-out methods of his rival.

But the lane will turn, and it's a long worm that has no turning, or whatever the proverb says. Also the thickest skin has a quick place under it if only you stick the pin deep enough. Speaking of skins, Dave Howell was a pachyderm. Now and then, though, there were surface indications that Ellick's pin had found somebody at home. After one particularly vicious thrust the coarse laughter of the crowd had been prolonged by the sight of the victim's face, which had gone white instead of red, while the lips tightened and the warm sparkle of the black eyes turned to a cold glint.

"I 'lowed fer a minute Lyin' Dave was about to git his fightin' britches on," Jeff Lawson confided to Marcus Green, his bunk-mate, as they laced their boots next morning.

"Naw, Jeff," Marcus declared oracularly. "Lyin' Dave's fightin' britches is locked up in his trunk, an' the key's lost! That feller'll take anything offen anybody."

Little did the rough but kindly men of Camp Six dream that tragic events impended, under whose sobering stress all petty animosities would be forgotten in a moment. All the long, hot Sunday afternoon the crews sat outside the bunk-house, smoking, playing cards, nailing massive half-soles on worn boots, or mending harness. Jim Roberts, the boss, had taken the little narrow-gauge engine, Number Nine, with three men, including Dave Howell, to inspect a new trestle thrown across a ravine near the upper end of the line.

Draggin' Ellick sat on a rude bench at the shady end of the house, from which position he commanded a view up the track. The heat waves from the rails shimmered in the broiling sun. Ellick seemed to be only smoking and dozing, but in reality he was in the throes of cogitation, trying to frame some yet more subtle and mirth-provoking persiflage than had ever fallen upon the responsive ears of his loyal constituents.

Suddenly a figure appeared far up the track, rounding the curve at a rapid walking gait. In a moment the characteristic slue-footed list identified the walker as Dave Howell. For so hot a day Dave was certainly making good time. "Wonder what's a-pushin' Lyin' Dave," called out one of the skidder crew. "He's shore workin' the ol' skew-leg fer all hit's wuth!"

"Let's git him started on one of his big yarns," said another, and at the suggestion an evil smile lurked on Draggin' Ellick's ruddy face.

"That's a plumb good idy, boys," he said. "I'll banter him to do hisself proud this time, an' then I've jest thought of a brand-new drag I'll git off on him."

And scenting the battle from afar, the gang began instinctively to close in round the champion. As soon as Dave's sprightly limp brought him within hailing distance, Hendrix sang out: "Hey thar, Lyin' Dave, light an' rest yer saddle! Come an' git ye a cheer an' set down by it, an' tell us the biggest lie ye ever heard. We're jest a-pinin' away, like, fer to hear a whoppin' big un!"

But a glance at Dave's face showed that it was on no errand of mirth-making he had come. Tragedy was written there. He didn't even smile at the jester's words, but staggered to a place in the center of the group, where he stood panting, a breathless herald of important tidings.

"Fellers, they's trouble back up yander! Number Nine busted through that thar trustle at the Gap, an' Jim Roberts is a-lyin' under her, pinned agin a pile of cross-ties. He can talk, though, an' he said fer Ellick to git a crew of the best men in camp an' fetch axes an' block an' tackle, so's ye can h'ist the tracks offen him. Hit'll be three hours afore the wreckin' train can git up thar."

Instantly Camp Six was astir. Stalwart men, chosen by Hendrix, nearly ran over each other in their haste to grab ropes, pulleys and axes. Ellick was a dozen

Courtesy of the Great Smoky Mountains National Park   Photographed by Jim Shelton
Lumber train with skidder on a trestle up Lynn Camp Prong.

yards ahead of all the rest when the relief party set out on the six-mile walk. He was not a walker as most mountaineers are, but he felt complimented that the boss, in his hour of need, had recognized him as the man to pick a crew and come to the rescue. He therefore took the lead all the way, albeit with vast expenditure of wind and water, for he was panting like a farrier's bellows and sweating like a leaky barrel.

"Come on as fast as ye can, boys," he stopped now and then to urge, the while he mopped his steaming brow and caught his breath in stertorous heavings. "We've got to keep a-hittin' the grit an' help the boss out o' trouble. An' I reckon I've been a leetle too rough on Lyin' Dave. He was might'-nigh give out when he got to camp, but he said he'd foller us back as soon as be blowed a spell. I 'low I'll let up on draggin' him so hard, seein' how game he's showed hisself."

Suddenly the Sabbath stillness of the mountains was broken by the shriek of a locomotive from somewhere up the gorge. The weird swelling of the shrill notes indicated that the engine was approaching. The men stopped in amazement. There was no log train in the woods today. The wrecker could not arrive from Beechmont in less than two hours from now. And Number Nine was lying wrecked in a ravine two miles above.

"What in thunder do you make of that, Ellick?" Wilse Anderson asked between his labored gasps for wind. "Them fellers couldn't 'a' got old Nine on the track by theirselves, could they?"

"Why, gosh, no! Of course they couldn't. Hit's got me guessin' fer shore," Ellick admitted. "Let's go on; we'll be findin' out somethin' afore long now."

They pressed on again, but had gone less than a hundred yards before they heard the whistle again, this time much nearer. As they stood still a moment, puzzling over the strange situation, the rumble of the approaching engine was heard, and in a few minutes the familiar head end of Number Nine nosed round a sharp curve toward camp, and when Hendrix flagged her with his red bandanna handkerchief the engineer brought her to a stop where the relief crew stood.

"Whar in thunder air you-uns headed fer? Huntin' a bee tree?" Jim Roberts asked as he leaned out of the cab window beside the engineer.

"Boss, how in the name of Tom Walker did you git her back on the rails? Was ye hurt bad?" Ellick asked in reply.

"Git *who* back on the rails? Was *who* hurt? What are you-uns a-talkin' about? Ye must 'a' found a stillhouse instid of a bee tree!" Roberts shot back.

Then Draggin' Ellick began to see light. "What did you fellers do with Lyin' Dave?"

"Why, we didn't do nothin' with him. After we started up to look at the new trestle we found we were crowded in this little box of a cab, and I let him get off a mile from camp and walk back," the boss exclaimed. "Did anything happen to him?"

"Hit hain't happened to him yit, Boss!" And Draggin' Ellick rose painfully from the stump on which he had dropped to rest.

Then the men in the cab and the sweating huskies on the ground began also to see the light. First they grinned foolishly, then they chuckled, and then they roared until the rocky cañon walls roared back at them. And Draggin' Ellick did just what most inveterate jokers do when the laugh comes the other way. He got mad, not just peeved or provoked or indignant—mad; mad all over. He was so mad he couldn't talk; he couldn't even cuss. He sputtered. Then he clambered up on the tender with the rest of the crew, and sputtered while Number Nine coasted into camp.

The men at the camp were lined up in front of the mess shack as the would-be rescuers and the would-have-been rescued climbed off the engine. It was a joyous reception. The big roughnecks squealed and howled and bellowed their delight.

But Draggin' Ellick scanned the faces in the crowd for one that was conspicuously missing. "Whar's that thar low-down lyin' skunk?" he shouted above the unabating chorus of mirth.

"He done went an' gone from here, Ellick," Jeff Lawson replied, with happy tears still streaking his face. "He said he had a good job waitin' fer him with the Ca'liny Spruce, an' he 'lowed hit was a good time to go an' git it. But thar's his compliments he axed us to give ye, to remember him by." And he pointed to a placard crudely lettered on a cracker-box lid tacked above the mess-shack door. It read:

To Draggin Ellick
good by pardner
sorry i cudent think of no biger
lye to tell ye. the feller that
drags last drags the furdest.

SIMPLE IKE'S DAUGHTER

Simple Ike's gal. So the Tucker's Cove folk called her. Not unkindly, though, for nobody thought unkindly of Maybelle Gaby. Nor of her father, for that matter. Ike Gaby wasn't to blame for being "simple." Some people are just born that way. Sort of dispensation of Providence, as pious folks say.

To be sure, there was difference of opinion in Tucker's Cove as to whether Ike Gaby *was* simple. Mountain folk haven't such infallible yardsticks for measuring the human mind as our glib professors of education have nowadays. In Tucker's Cove we just look at a fellow and listen to his talk, then form our own opinion as to how much brains and hoss sense Godamighty gave him.

As far as looks went, Ike Gaby's were against him. The short stretch of forehead between his black foretop and his bushy eyebrows certainly didn't suggest a giant intellect. Nor was his talk any more in his favor than his looks. His tongue and lips struggled hard with vowels and consonants, and his stuttering speech was scarcely intelligible.

Everybody knew, too, that despite several terms of schooling Ike had never so much as learned his letters. The gawky boy with his perpetual grin had gulped and sputtered at the foot of class after class in the Possum Trot school, the despair of his teachers and the source of perennial mirth to the other children.

Then came Noah Dilrod to be the "perfesser" at Possum Trot. Noah had all the qualifications of a good schoolmaster except such minor ones as scholarship, common sense, sympathy, and understanding of children. The essentials he had in abundance: a powerful frame, a raucous voice, a domineering manner, and a pull with the district directors. He kept school in Tucker's Cove for two dreary decades.

Noah Dilrod endured Ike Gaby's pathetic efforts for three days. In that time he had psychoanalyzed the lad—though that fine new word hadn't yet been invented. He brought a heavy hand palm-down upon the desk with a bang that made every tiny tad draw in his head like a terrapin.

"Pick up yer books, big boy, an' git fer home! If the Good Lord had meant fer you to git an eddication, He'd have give you brains to git it with. Nobody can eddicate an *idjit*!"

The children winced, partly for terror, partly for pity, but Ike Gaby only grinned. Slowly he gathered his battered speller, primer, and slate and rose to go.

"Yeth thir, Pefether, g-g-geth ye're right," he mumbled as plainly as his clumsy mouth could emit the words. "I kn-n-nowed somethin' matter—g-g-geth that 'th it—j-j-jist a b-b-borned idjit!" And the grin exploded into a cackle that made the children stick their heads out again as the ungainly boy slipped out the door.

Thus ended the academic career of Ike Gaby. Never again were his poor eyes to be mocked and tortured by the cruel symbols of Cadmus, the Phoenician. Letters and figures in books were not for him. Henceforth he belonged to the great world of out-of-doors. He *could* see the big elemental things of *that* world—hills, trees, rocks, cattle, and the like. These were made for such eyes as his. These things he could understand.

Hills, trees, rocks, cattle. Especially cattle. Ike Gaby had a way with cattle. Cows and calves, beef-steers, draft-oxen, they were things he could make sense of. He never tired of tending them on the range. On his father's rocky hillside farm there was a fair-sized herd of them. They needed a husky fellow to mend fences, carry salt to the licks on the grassy balds, now and then to take the dogs and chase a bear back to the deep woods.

Shortly after Ike's "quituation" from Noah Dilrod's school, he was left an orphan with the farm and the bunch of yearlings on the pasturage. The neighbors wondered how Ike could ever manage to shift for himself, but somehow he seemed to get along.

In fact, he soon showed signs of becoming what his father aspired to be but never was—a born trader. It was hard to understand his mumbling jargon when he would accost a neighbor, but sooner or later he would make it clear that he was wanting to buy, sell, or swap a cow-brute or a beef-critter. And the canniest Scotch-Irish hillsman in the Cove had to admit that Ike could dicker shrewdly with the best of them.

"Simple Ike shore knows beast-es," was the usual comment. "Can't fool him on nothin' that goes on the hoof."

Before long Ike had the best-stocked cattle range in the county. Patient industry, almost uncanny judgment, and trading sense had made him the pride and the envy of Tucker's Cove.

Never once, though, did he even question the verdict pronounced upon him by Noah Dilrod. Any fool, he knew, that hasn't sense enough to learn readin', writin' an' cipherin' is tetched in the head. All he was fit for was to stick on the farm, raise calves, fatten them, sell them, and buy more calves. Most anybody can do that, Ike 'lowed.

About this time Polly Judson, accompanied by her father, a "widder-man," moved into Tucker's Cove. And Polly was comely enough to be restful to the eyes of any man. She had sense, too; had gone through high school and taken a course in the business college at Crockettsburg. She was keeping books for the

Crockettsburg Racket Store when her father felt the call of the hills and bought the farm adjoining Ike Gaby's.

Polly started in to raise chickens, ducks, and turkeys to keep life in the shut-in cove from being intolerable. Then she bought a calf or two from Ike Gaby. She found him a friendly sort, a good neighbor, after she learned to understand his labored speech. In his awkward way he told her things she needed to know—how to judge, buy, condition, and market calves. What to do when a steer was sick or a bossy was to be weaned. Every week she had need of his advice and his gladly proffered help.

Polly Judson was human, and lonely. Crockettsburg had been only a village, but Tucker's Cove was a barren island of loneliness in a vast ocean of billowy blue solitude. Gradually she grew more gratefully aware of the big, honest, kindly soul of her one real neighbor, and more strangely blind to his unprepossessing exterior.

When they were married Tucker's Cove chuckled a bit, but took it philosophically.

"Ike's outmarried hisself," people said. "He's shore got him a looker!"

"Yeah, but then agin, *she* mought 'a' done a heap wuss," another would argue. "Ike ain't no scholar ner no purty man, but he's well fixed an' he'll be good to his woman."

Polly made a dutiful and diligent mistress of the old Gaby homestead. The rambling log house was kept as clean as soap, water and scouring-sand could make it. The cattle throve, multiplied, brought good prices. Polly had a hankering for pretty things, a taste remarkably fine for one in her station. Ike was generous, and provided "fixin's" as willingly as provender. Polly put the touch of beauty upon them all. And she loved her man.

For all that, Polly had her hours of anxiety and foreboding before the year was out. What would her little one look like? Would his eyes be straight, his head well formed? Would he stand among men, shapely and good to look upon? What mother never hoped her son would be an Apollo?

The night Maybelle was born Polly's anguish was not mostly of the body. A strange fear clutched at her heart, a fear she could not disclose even to her husband. Even when the toothless midwife held the babe close for the young mother's first look and declared garrulously that "hit was as purty a gal baby as she'd ever in life seed borned," Polly wasn't quite trustful of the dim light of the kerosene lamp. She agonized until the full light of day broke, then tremblingly drew back the cover from the tiny head nestling in the hollow of her arm.

It was true! Every bit true! Her daughter, Ike Gaby's daughter, was without spot or blemish, as nearly perfect in trunk, limbs, and head as any madonna yearned for.

The ageless miracle of the chromosomes! Out of the millions of possible combinations, lovely or hideous, in the eternal lottery of Destiny, which the scholars call Heredity, there had been shaken together as fair and harmonious an assortment as ever falls into the laps of the daughters of men. With a sigh that was almost a moan, so surcharged it was with relief and the sheer joy of new motherhood, Polly sank back upon the pillow and sobbed herself into blissful sleep.

Despite her joy, however, a joy that was to grow with the passing weeks and years, Polly herself was never to know full health again. It was all she could do to drag about the house, care for the child, and give occasional attention to the flowers and chickens. Ike was good, though, and there was always a hired woman in the kitchen, so that Polly could spend most of her time "settin'."

Very busy "settin'" it was, to be sure, and Maybelle had all the care any baby could need. Polly did a hundred things that mountain mothers have no time to do for their offspring. With just the right touch of guidance she directed Maybelle's tottering steps, her prattling speech, her play, her happy bursts of song.

And every day she read to her. Polly had three whole shelves of books—more books than Tucker's Cove folk had even seen in one house. Queer a body would be bothered with such a mess of books. *Too* many books, they said. Nobody could read so much and be healthy.

"If Mis' Gaby had 'a' let them ol' books alone an' kep' out in the field with a hoe, she'd 'a' been a heap stouter today," the wise dames averred. "She's goin' to spile the youngun, too. Gals ort to make a hand in the corn an' tobacker agin they're eight or ten year old, instid of settin' an' listenin' to so much plumb foolishness out o' books."

Nevertheless, Maybelle grew up sturdy, brown legged, clear-eyed, vibrant with the up-bubbling of life. Her daddy grinned with delight at her childish ways. He listened to Polly's reading in the evenings, dumbly comprehending some of the simpler words. He never interrupted to ask questions about what he didn't understand. Maybelle understood, and that was enough. Looked as if she would grow up smart like her maw. That was his hope in life.

A day came when strange things happened at Possum Trot school. The drab one-room shack was abandoned and a new six-room building rose farther down the valley. The Cove people grumbled at the extravagance of putting good tax money into such costly structures just to teach younguns in, but the building was there, and nothing to be done about it.

Strangest of all, Noah Dilrod was not the "perfesser" in the new school. Rumor had it that he had failed to secure the necessary "stificate" and, therefore, couldn't ever teach any more. Seemed a shame and a pity. Noah had a big family and needed the money. Moreover, his arm was as strong as ever and his voice could still inspire terror as of yore. Better have let well enough alone.

Dilrod's successor, styled the "principal" instead of the "perfesser," was a dapper young man with a virginal mustache and a diploma from the State College. His five assistants were young women, the first of their sex ever employed to teach in Tucker's Cove. How they hoped to render bridlewise the untamed human colts and fillies of the settlement the old ones couldn't figure out. "Hit takes a heap more'n book-larnin' an' a sheepskin from a college to beat common sense into the younguns nowadays."

Despite the doubts of the wiseacres, however, the new principal, G. Adolphus Langston, and his fair colleagues got the school under way in short order. The rule of the hickory gave place to a regime of orthodox methodology. All the procedures of the past were as extinct as the five-toed horse.

The teachers talked about retardation and acceleration, mean and median, upper and lower quartile, intelligence quotient, and much else that would have been Greek to Noah Dilrod and Hebrew to Ike Gaby and his neighbors. The young staff was dead in earnest and pored nightly over books and notebooks. The one book they had studied least was the Book of the Living Child, that mystic volume wherein the wisest pedagogs have as yet turned but the first few pages.

Maybelle was seven. And school was to begin tomorrow. Her daddy had already bought her a first reader, a writing tablet, and a striped pencil box. Next morning, though, her mother was sick. Sicker than she had ever been. Ike sent for a doctor, who came on horseback toward evening. The doctor said she ought to be in a hospital, but she was too ill to make the journey.

Maybelle couldn't start to school the first day. And the next day Polly was worse. She lingered three weeks and on a Sunday she died. When Maybelle was finally ready to enter school, she was a whole month late.

Ike himself brought her. For years he had looked forward to the day when he should lead his daughter to enter in triumph the portals from which he had emerged in defeat. To prove that a Gaby could learn those baffling ABC's—that would be the proudest achievement of his life. It would be worth more than a hundred head of fat steers.

G. Adolphus Langston met them at the entrance. The grizzled father and the shrinking child followed him through the corridor, and stood embarrassed in his office.

"A new pupil to enter school?" the principal asked briskly. "Pretty late, I fear. But fill out this registration card for her."

Ike shook his head and struggled to explain his desire to become a patron of the school. It was plain enough to Langston that the fellow didn't know what it was all about. So he addressed himself to the girl.

"Name? Address? ...Why, that means where you live, of course. Father's name? Father's occupation? Ever attended school before? You *believe* not! Why, you surely *know* whether you ever went to school, don't you?"

Frightened by the newness of it all, by the crisp manner and rapid articulation of the stranger, Maybelle had to have several of the questions repeated. Meanwhile Langston was making mental notes. Fresh from a senior course in Abnormal Psychology, he recalled that low intelligence is in general hereditary, in accordance with the law of Mendel. Or at least that was what the books said.

"Very low I. Q.," he said to himself. "Much like 'Case D' in Van Toppel's new book, Diagnosis of the Sub-normal Child."

He touched an electric button and one of the assistants appeared.

"Miss Cowan, here is a girl who is going to require some special case study—a problem child, you know. Please bring me one of those diagnostic tests."

For more than an hour the child underwent the ordeal. With clocklike precision Langston plied her with questions and, watch in hand, checked her answers.

It was mainly the watch that proved Maybelle's undoing. She couldn't imagine why the man was in such a hurry. Most of the questions were simple enough and she could have answered them if he hadn't kept his eye on the dial all the time. Nobody in Tucker's Cove ever asked questions so fast or had to have answers so quickly. Cove folk answer slowly. People who talk too soon often get into trouble by it, so the old-timers say.

When the test was over Langston and Miss Cowan went over the papers and computed the score, while Maybelle and her father waited in the outer office.

"Just as I anticipated," the principal declared finally. "Sub-normal, that's all we can call her. No use of admitting her to school."

"But, Mr. Langston," the assistant began in a mild protest, "she certainly doesn't look or talk like a feeble-minded child. Maybe conditions weren't just right—she was painfully timid and self-conscious, as you noticed, and—"

"Tut, tut, Miss Cowan. This test is the last word in mental measurements. We can't let a kindly sentiment influence us in the face of science."

"But, Mr. Langston, shouldn't we give her a chance? I can't bear to see the suffering that's going to be in that child's face when you tell her she can't come to school."

"Pshaw, Miss Cowan, a defective child like this is incapable of feeling disappointment or humiliation as a normal child would."

Reluctantly Miss Cowan yielded to the authority of her superior. She remained in the room when Maybelle was summoned.

The girl heard the verdict without a tear, without even a tremor in her voice as she rose to go.

"All right, sir; Dad said you would know what was best. Of course, sir, I've wanted to come more than I ever wanted anything in the world, but if I can't—"

"That's all right, youngster," Langston broke in with a laugh. "We can't all be scholars, you know. It takes all kinds of people to make a world."

"Yes, sir, that's what Dad says. He says there are other ways to live besides going to school. I'll just try to quit wanting to go."

Hurt beyond all weeping, Maybelle dragged her heavy feet and heavier heart up the homeward road. Ike understood, and strode beside her in speechless sympathy. When they reached the gate at home he took her in his arms and carried her up the lower-bordered path.

"'At's aw right, honey! D-d-don't keer what the Perfether said. Ye're jes' as s-smart as anybody's gal. B-b-but you an' I k-kin git along 'thout no ol' school."

Courtesy of the Great Smoky Mountains National Park   Photographed by Edouard E. Exline

Class in session at the Little Greenbrier School - 1936.

"'Deed we can, Daddy. You did and I can. And I'm going to learn to read by my own self. Mother taught me some of the littlest words, and I'll learn a lot more. Some day I'll read all her books to you!"

Ike grinned, though it was but to hide his heartbreak.

But there were many things Ike didn't know; and the greatest of these was Maybelle.

From that day she set herself with indomitable will to the staggering task of learning to read without a teacher. Every day, between chores in kitchen and yard, she would curl up in the armchair by the window with one of her mother's story-books. Laboriously she would puzzle out the words Polly had shown her. To this little stock she slowly added a few others by association. They came with difficulty at first, but a bit more easily as the days went by.

Every week now she had more words. And such beautiful words they were. All lovely things, and lovely words most of all, were food and drink to her hungering soul. Before long she was able to read the simplest stories connectedly. And each victory gave her new confidence, new power to acquire more words and larger meanings. Soon she was reading stories at sight—reading them aloud to her dear daddy.

Ike would sit by her side, smiling in dumb rapture as he listened. A Gaby reading a book! It seemed unreal, impossible. He half suspected it wasn't really-truly reading—just play-like reading, too likely. Why, not even a *smart* man's child could learn to read without even going to school and being taught the ABC's! Poor child, though, he wouldn't discourage her for the world. Let her *think* she could read, anyhow.

The years came and went. The calves grew and fattened. Father and daughter lived and toiled, saved and prospered. They enjoyed the friendship of their neighbors, and the old house was not without its share of guests.

Best of all, though, were the long evenings when nobody came. Maybelle had read and re-read all her mother's books and now bought new ones of her own. Ike was a rapt and responsive listener. By slow degrees his cabined mind had gained in power to understand. With her he outgrew the childish fancies of the little primers and thrilled to the tales of the Arabian Nights, the Adventures of Robinson Crusoe, and the colorful iliads and odysseys of the wide world's Homeridae. Books of history, travel, and biography evoked grunts of wonder and chuckles of delight that lingered in his dreams at night and echoed in his memory on the grassy ranges on the morrows.

Noah Dilrod and G. Adolphus Langston were conversing at the crossroads store. Ike and Maybelle were taking their departure after their weekly shopping trip. Dilrod, flattered by a word of recognition from the man who had supplanted him at Possum Trot, was in a friendly mood.

"Thar goes Idjit Ike Gaby an' his gal. I reckon ye've heared of 'em."

"Yes, I met them some time ago. A pathetic case. The girl is bright-looking enough, dresses neatly, and outwardly seems a normal child. I gave her a careful test, however, and found her a moron. Of course, I had to exclude her from school."

"Ye done right, Mr. Langston," agreed the ex-perfesser. "Hit's in the breed. Her daddy come to *my* school twenty year ago an' I shipped him the third day. Us school-teachers can't afford to fool away our time tryin' to eddicate idjits!"

JEFF HOWELL'S BURYIN'

It was the strangest funeral ever held in Galax Cove. Two groups of mourners glowered at each other across the open grave. Behind them a little distance an outer circle of mountain neighbors huddled nervously in the rustic churchyard. In the center of each of the two inner groups sobbed a young woman holding a babe at her breast. The strange thing about it was that each of the two women knew herself to be the wife of Jeff Howell, whose body was even now being lowered into the grave. And each knew Jeff Howell was the father of her babe.

The dead man's father and mother and a score of kinsmen stood grim-faced beside Louviny, whom all Galax had seen married to Jeff by Preacher Pleas Ballard. Louviny's tears rolled unrestrained down her cheeks, some of them raining upon the face of her now fatherless child.

The other woman, too, was surrounded by a bodyguard, strangers all in Galax, who had come with her bringing Jeff's body across Big Piney from the lumber camp on Nolichucky, where Jeff had been working and where he had been killed in a sawmill accident.

"This here's Minnie, yer son's woman, and his baby, an' I'm her uncle," the oldest of the Nolichucky cortege had abruptly announced when the wagons had brought the corpse and the sad tiding to the parental cabin.

There ensued a stormy scene, of course, with angry threats and counter-threats, as another age-old "triangle" was pieced out, with its fifty-mile base-line stretched across the mountain divide and its apex—well, that was lying out there in a wagon, in a crude pine coffin.

"Hit won't never do to let them two women git together, or they'll be hell a-poppin' all over the place," the cooler heads had cautioned, and Minnie had been hurried away to a neighbor's house for the night. The rest of the Nolichucky folk had likewise been provided lodgings as far as possible from the house of mourning.

Even at that, there were muttered hints of a "ruction." The keening of the women at the "wake" that night was made more harrowing by the forebodings of mothers, sisters, and wives over what was likely to happen at the burying on the morrow.

Soon after daybreak they sent a horse and buggy to the head of the creek to bring Preacher Pleas Ballard. He was the patriarch, priest, and prophet of Galax Cove. Ninety years of age, stone-blind, and all but bedfast with palsy, he was seldom seen in the valley any more, but when there was trouble, when the shadow of fear fell over the dark mountain slopes, they always sent for Preacher

Pleas. He had come again today. They carried him in his chair and placed him near the head of the grave, and he sat leaning upon his gnarled staff, his sightless eyes blinking in the afternoon sun.

When the plow lines with which the coffin was lowered had been pulled up, coiled, and laid aside, a few spadefuls of clods rattled down upon the covering-boards, and then the crowd stood with bared heads. Nothing broke the stillness save the weeping of Louviny and Minnie, but the air was surcharged with impending tragedy. On both sides of the waiting grave hardset jaws, and cold, unblinking eyes seemed only waiting for a signal. At any moment either woman, bursting out in a bitter accusation or angry challenge, might give that signal.

"All ready, Uncle Pleas," someone whispered.

Pleas Ballard could neither read nor write, but when he prayed it was as if he conversed with One who stood and listened. He knew no "Thou" nor "Thee" but addressed the Almighty respectfully as one gentleman might another.

Pleas Ballard prayed.

Courtesy of the Great Smoky Mountains National Park   Photographed by Harry Wolfe

Proffitt Cemetery around 1930. Notice the practice of mounding the graves and decorating with crepe paper and tissue paper flowers and drapings.

"We're here, Sir, to bury a pore boy we thought a heap of. A nice young man he was, Sir, an' we're sorry he had to go so suddent. We hate it mighty bad he didn't allus do the right thing. The last time I seed him, about a month ago, I reckon, he come up an' told me about the sorry mess he'd got his self an' two good weemen into. He was jest a pore weak mountain boy, Sir, an' he was sufferin' a livin' hell.

"We hope he got it fixed up with you, Sir, afore he was took. But we want you to take pity on these here two young weemen with their babes. Hit's human nater fer 'em to be full of hate an' pizen feelins agin each other. You know how that is, Sir. But what's been done can't be undone, an' we want ye to help 'em fergit an' fergive. Them's two mighty sweet words, Sir, they air. Help these pore young widder women to fergive him that's dead, an' fergive each other. Thanky, Sir. Amen!"

The menfolk put on their hats again, the outer circle moved softly inward, and the two groups at the graveside had somehow melted into one, with silent shaking of hands all round. Louviny and Minnie meanwhile edged closer, as all the men took turns shoveling the earth into the grave.

Suddenly, in an ancient symbolism of the hill country, each woman, without a word, held out her own babe to the other and for a brief moment clasped the other woman's child to her own bared breast, marble-white against the folds of her "mourning dress." Louviny was the first to speak.

"If ye'll come an' take the night with me, Minnie, I'll be right proud to have ye."

WHITE MULE

The peaceful haze of a perfect autumn morning lay upon the Unakas, but the heart of Magalene Cagle was not at peace. The half grown mountain girl stood beside a huge wooden-hooped churn, and her sturdy brown arms plied the dasher vigorously up and down in the shade of the old log spring house; but Magalene's mind was not on her churning.

Now and then she turned to cast an anxious glance toward the weather-beaten house that stood at a little distance. The smoke of Maw Cagle's breakfast fire still curled lazily from the stone chimney, and her whining voice could be heard as she directed the younger children to their morning tasks.

It was not about her mother, however, that Magalene was troubled, but about her father. Amos Cagle was reputed a hard-working, quiet-spoken citizen and an exemplary husband and parent. For all that Magalene, his first-born, was worried about him.

For three weeks or more she had been keeping a solicitous eye upon his movements. Morning after morning she had seen him leave the house after breakfast and, with his rifle on his shoulder, stalk up the twisting trail that led to nowhere in particular, as far as anybody knew. He was supposed to be working on a contract to get out chestnut telephone poles; but in her ten years Magalene had observed that pole cutters usually took axes to the woods, instead of rifles.

Once she had ventured to question her mother on the subject, but the tired-faced, meek-eyed mountain woman had shut her up almost fiercely.

" 'Tain't none o' yore business to be projeckin' into yer pappy's doin's. You 'tend to yourn an' he'll look after hisn. I hain't never axed him what he's a doin', an' I don't aim to."

That was Tildy Cagle's wifely philosophy. Like many another dutiful spouse in the hills, she would keep her man's secrets as close as a tomb whenever he chose to divulge them to her. Were he in hiding as an outlaw or fugitive from the pursuing law, she would come to him with food or tidings at peril of her life; but never would she question him as to his plans.

"I don't know what he 'lows to do. I hain't heard him name hit"—so speaks the Penelope of the Unakas.

Magalene, however, had a queer habit of thinking things out for herself. Perhaps it was because she was nearly ten years old, the eldest of eight children, and partly also because she had been "out" to school for two years, and had picked up ideas and notions about various things. At any rate she kept eyeing the barnyard gate as she tended the churn, and the little furrow of anxiety between her hazel eyes grew deeper as she waited.

Presently her ears caught the bumping of wheels on the loose stones, and a moment later her father's old canvas-topped wagon, drawn by two rawboned bays, rumbled out of the barn lot. Amos drew rein by the spring house and climbed down from his seat under the arch of the wagon bows.

"Be a good gal, Magalene, an' he'p yer mammy all ye can," he said with a kindliness that belied the gruffness of his tone. "If I sell my load to-day, I'll try to fetch ye some purties—maybe a new dress an' them stockin's ye been wantin'."

The girl smiled, but her voice was close to tears as she spoke. "What kind of load ye takin', pap?" she inquired.

"About twenty-five bushel of apples," the man replied, as he took up a link in the trace chain of the off horse.

"I thought ye said t'other day the apples was sich a sorry crap this year ye didn't aim to wagon 'em to town," the girl argued.

"They ain't much, fer a fact, but they'll bring a little bit o' cash money—better'n lettin' 'em lay an' rot."

"I'm afeared they won't bring enough to pay fer haulin' 'em, pap, sayin' nothin' of buyin' no dresses an' things. I don't want ye should bother 'bout bringin' *me* nothin'."

"Well, we'll jes' wait an' see how hit comes out," Amos answered. He was in the act of mounting to his seat again when he suddenly turned. "Aw, shucks!" he exclaimed. "I was fergittin' somethin'. I'll have to go up to the sheep house in the upper deadenin' an' git a half bushel to measure these here apples in. Jes' tend the hosses while I'm gone, Magalene, an' don't let nobody come messin' around the load. I'll be back in fifteen minutes."

Courtesy of the Great Smoky Mountains National Park
Photographed by Charles S. Grossman
Churning Butter - 1937.

Left on guard with the wagon and team, the girl went back to her churn, a dozen steps away. The butter had come and she began to dress the golden-yellow mass and press it into the wooden molds. She washed her hands at the spring branch and dried them on her apron. Then a sudden curiosity seized her.

"Maw'd break my neck, I reckon, but I'm p'intedly bound to take one look," she said to herself.

Stepping to the back of the wagon with furtive haste, she thrust her hands under the wagon sheet and into the bundles of fodder that lined the rough bed in which the apples were piled. The apples, she saw at a glance, were miserably faulty and bruised. They would be nothing but cider pomace after being jolted over the twenty miles of rocks and ruts that led to Crockettsburg, the county seat village.

In a moment, however, the girl's fingers touched something else. She did not need to uncover the hard object to know what it was—a two-gallon stone jug corked with a short length of corncob. A second later she felt another jug, and then a third. She drew the nearest one close and bent toward it with her nose. The eloquent fragrance of the saturated corncob stopper told her all she cared to know.

"So pap's went an' tuck to blockadin'!" she muttered, trembling with excitement, and with something between terror and anger. "Them's the telephone poles he's been gittin' out!"

Grimly she replaced the covering of fodder blades. Going to the spring, she set a crock containing the new-made butter on a flat stone in the cold water. Then she brought out two large empty milk jars and placed them beside the churn. She could not keep back the big tears that rolled down her cheeks and fell upon the grass.

"What's got into pap?" she asked herself. "He's allus hated the name of a blockader. I never dremp' he'd git into hit. Hit don't never git nobody in nothin' but trouble—he ought to have sense enough to know that!"

Then, as if conscience-smitten after such an outburst of unfilial indignation, she continued her half audible soliloquy in a sobbing undertone.

"Pore pap! Ever'thing on this here tore-down ol' place has went bad fer him this year. The freeze killed the fruit, the big tide washed the hay away, the drought ruined the tobacker, an' the cholery killed most of the fattenin' hawgs. On top of that, ol' Cam Briggs talked pap into goin' his security on that note, an' then pulled out an' left him to pay twelve hundred dollars at the bank. 'Tain't much wonder he tuck up with moonshinin', but hit's goin' to land him in the jail house!"

She rinsed the heavy jars with fresh water. Magalene could think better when her hands were busy.

"I know he don't like this business nary bit better'n I do," she went on. "He's doin' hit jes' so's he can give maw an' us younguns a chance. Six gallon o' white corn liquor—ten dollar a gallon—law, hit's wuth more'n them wormy apples an' the ol' wagon throwed in! I reckon he *could* git me some purties if he sold hit, an' the good Lord knows I need 'em!"

Magalene glanced down at her ragged skirt and her bare, shapely legs, golden-brown from a summer of stockingless exposure to sun and wind.

"An' maw an' Virgie an' Rutheeny an' all the balance is as nigh naked as I am," she said.

Far up the mountainside, at that moment, she saw her father striding across the deadening toward the sheep house. He would be back in a few minutes; and at the thought of his setting out on his first dangerous journey as a purveyor of illicit "mountain dew," her tears started afresh.

"I'd ruther than a million dollars he wouldn't 'a' got into this! I'd ruther wear these old' rags till they fell plumb off o' me!"

Then a sudden light of decision shone in her face, and she dried her eyes with one of the few unsoiled spots in her apron.

"I ain't goin' to see my pap buy me no clo'es with blockade money," she declared. "An' he ain't goin' to no jail house to-night if I can he'p it!"

In the outskirts of the straggling village of Crockettsburg stood an old wooden building, which, having gone the way of all good livery stables, was now a combination of filling station, garage, and black-smith shop, known as Phil's Place. Its red-lettered sign admonished the passing motorists to "Stop and Fill with Phil."

There were, it may be said, underground rumors afloat to the effect that this cordial invitation to the fleeting traveler might on occasion suggest the replenishing of dry receptacles other than gasoline tanks. To the wiseacres of the village, at least it seemed hardly credible that the amazing popularity of Phil's Place with the tourists who slowed down and stopped there was wholly attributable to the superiority of its gas and oil or the exceptional skill of Phil Forbush, the grizzled proprietor, who was really a blacksmith by tradition and training and a garage owner by force of circumstances.

The front of the converted livery stable, facing the highway, was usually filled with cars and motorists. The rear end opened upon an enclosed space known as the "swappin' lot," and used as the rendezvous of the mountain farmers who came in their covered wagons for "truckin' an' tradin'." Phil's Place had thus become the meeting point for the rubber-tired present and the steel-tired past, and was the busiest spot in the sleepy municipality of Crockettsburg.

It was high noon when Amos Cagle's apple schooner, with all canvas set, sailed into the haven of the "swappin' lot." Phil Forbush, always on the alert to adjust a carburetor or supply a hamestring, approached, his leather apron flapping in the wind.

"Howdy, Amos? What fer ye to-day?" he inquired, with a professional glance at the horses' feet.

"Nothin' much, I reckon," Amos drawled. "Jes' drapped in to blow the hosses a minute. Needin' any apples—or somethin' thataway?"

"Guess not to-day," replied Phil. "Been several wagons in ahead of ye. Ye must 'a' got a late start this mornin'."

"Did. I'd ought to 'a' loaded up las' night. They ain't nothin' else ye'd be carin' fer, I reckon?"

Amos was trying to appear casual, but was awkwardly hesitant. A seasoned "shiner" would have carried it off with charming nonchalance, but Amos was a green hand.

Forbush looked at the mountaineer quizzically. He knew everybody who patronized his place, and what manner of cargo each was wont to bring.

"What else ye got, Amos? Some sarghum or tree molasses, or somethin'?"

"Yeah, somethin'."

By dint of considerable outward effort and with much inward trepidation, Amos managed to achieve an unmistakable wink. Phil's bewhiskered face cracked open with a broad grin that stretched into a hearty guffaw.

"Well, dad burn my hide, Amos! *You* hain't tuck to bilin' the ol' copper kettle of nights, have ye?"

"Had to do somethin' to keep from bein' sold out by the high sheriff," replied Amos soberly. "I don't favor hit, but hit's that or somethin' worse, times like these."

"Yeah, hit gits the best of 'em nowadays," Phil agreed; "but I'm sort o' hatin' to see ye follerin' hit, Amos. Hit's gittin' more dangerous here lately. They say they's revenooers workin' in this county right now, an' I'm lookin' to git raided 'most any day. I've quit storin' any stuff here. All I do is give some of these tourin' fellers the high sign an' let 'em do their own tradin' off o' some wagon that comes in. I'd shore hate to see *you* git in trouble."

"Yeah, I'd hate it myself. My women folks is turrible ag'in hit, specially the oldest gal. She hain't got no idee I ever made a drap; but a man's got to chance somethin' to git somethin'. I 'low I ain't likely to git cotch the fust time, anyhow."

The honk of a motor horn sounded from the front. Phil turned to wait upon a well-dressed stranger who had stepped out of a smart-looking roadster.

"Jes' you wait here, Amos, till I see what that feller wants," he ordered.

In a few minutes he returned with the stranger.

"Amos," he began, "here's a gent that's driv a right smart ways, an' he 'lows he might like a apple or somethin' to take the dust out o' his goozle. Maybe him an' you could do come tradin'."

The motorist glanced curiously at the mountaineer and his quaint outfit, and came to the point at once.

"Old man, I'm dry as a bone. Have you anything that's good for a large-sized thirst?"

"Mister," Amos confided, "I've got a leetle home-made medicine that's gorranteed fer that complaint."

"What do you call it?" queried the thirsty one, who was evidently a "furriner" from the distant world beyond the mountains.

"Hit's what a heap o' people calls white mule. Hit's made out o' corn."

"Is it absolutely pure?"

"Jest as pure an' purty an' white as was ever run into a jug, mister. Hit wouldn't hurt a sick man or a baby."

Amos had loosed the end gate of the wagon and brought forth one of the jugs. The stranger bent toward it, and the whiff from the corncob was evidently reassuring.

"All right, old man! I'll take the jug. How much is it?"

The canny Amos at this stage proceeded cautiously. "Well, I want jes' what's right an' fair. Course ye understand hit costs a right smart to make good stuff, an' likewise to haul hit sich a long ways. Resky, too, ye know."

"Certainly, I understand that," the outlander conceded. "Name your price. If it's right, we'll trade."

"Now, mister," Amos haggled in the true Scotch-Irish style, "you're a city man, an' ye know what the stuff fetches in town. I'd ruther ye'd make me a offer. I'm confident ye're a squar man."

"Well, I can buy all I want at ten dollars a gallon," the customer countered. "How does that strike you?"

"I 'low that's reasonable," assented Amos, with no outward betrayal of the satisfaction he inwardly felt. The purchaser drew a crisp twenty-dollar note from a roll and handed it to the mountaineer. Phil Forbush stood by, an interested spectator.

"That closes the trade, old man?" queried the stranger.

"Yes, sir, that seals hit tight, I reckon. Want me to tote the jug an' put hit in yer cyar?"

"No! Leave it where it is!" commanded the stranger in a sudden tone of authority. "And you stand still where *you* are. You're under arrest!"

Throwing open his coat, he exhibited the shiny badge of a deputy revenue collector. The crestfallen mountaineer gulped in astonishment. Then he began to see red.

"Ye infernal yaller hound!" he roared, and made a motion toward the wagon, where his rifle lay beneath the fodder under the seat.

"Steady, old man!" The officer's voice was cool and his manner ominously quiet. "You've made one mistake to-day. Don't make another!"

"No, Amos, don't try to start nothin'," the friendly Phil cautioned. "Hit's yer fust offense, an' the court ain't apt to give ye a heavy sentence. Jes' take hit ca'm."

"Ca'm the devil!" bellowed Amos, out of his senses with blind rage. "I sold ye what ye axed fer, at yer own figger. Ye durn sneakin', onrey reptile! Nobody but a low-born son—"

"Shet up, Amos!" ordered Phil sharply, being one who knew the inside as well as the outside of the situation. "Ye're actin' the fool an' ruinin' yer case. He hain't tuck ye with no warrant yit, ner told ye what ye're charged with. Talk civil to him!"

"We don't need any warrant," snapped the deputy. "I've caught the man with the goods on him."

"Ye hain't examined the goods yit," argued Phil.

"I guess I know corn liquor when I smell it! We'll just take another look, though, to clear up this gentleman's doubts. Get me a cup."

Forbush, greatly distressed both because of the raid on his own place and also because of a good neighbor's unhappy plight, hastened to his little office up front and returned quickly with a tumbler. He was followed by a score of patrons and hangers-on who had been tipped off as to what was going on. The officer took the glass and pulled hard at the redolent stopper of the jug, which came out with a noisy *poong*. Tipping the jug, he poured a small quantity of its contents into the tumbler.

Three separate and distinct gasps broke the dramatic silence that had fallen upon the group—one from the astonished representative of the law, one from the mystified proprietor, and one—the loudest of all—from the dumbfounded mountaineer.

"What in thunder?" demanded the officer.

"What the Sam Hill?" stammered Phil Forbush.

"What the devil an' Tom Walker?" sputtered Amos Cagle.

From the mouth of the jug trickled a foamy stream of snow-white buttermilk!

Amos was the first of the trio to regain his composure. In a second he was grinning amiably at the officer. "Ye see, mister, I was tellin' ye the God's truth. I said hit was the purest, purtiest, whitest stuff that was ever run into a jug. I told ye hit wouldn't hurt a sick man ner a baby!"

The deputy, however, was not to be duped by the old trick of one dummy container in a cargo of illicit spirits. He quickly fished out the two remaining jugs from the wagon and drew the stoppers. When they, too, had poured forth their milky libation he turned angrily upon Cagle.

"See here, my man, do you think you can put a job like that over on a Federal officer? Do you expect me to believe you came all the way from the mountains just to bring this load of rotten apples and a little buttermilk?"

"Well, mister," chuckled Amos, "if ye ain't satisfied with what ye've bought to quinch yer thirst with, here's yer twenty back. I wasn't aimin' to keep hit, nohow. I was jest a devilin' ye a little, not knowin' who ye was, an' you not troublin' to interdooce yerself."

By this time the spectators began to roar their mirth. It was apparent to them that Amos had perpetrated a clever practical joke upon a "revenooer"—a natural enemy of their species—and they were prepared to enjoy it to the limit. Then Phil Forbush, though he hadn't the slightest idea how it had all happened, saw his chance to complete the vindication of his friend, and incidentally to clear his own establishment from suspicion.

"Mister," he said, when the laughter had abated somewhat, "you must excuse me an' Amos fer havin' our devilmint. I've knowed Amos Cagle fer forty year—knowed his daddy before him. They never was a Cagle that I ever heared of that was a blockader. They're ag'in' it, same as I am. I wouldn't allow no man to fetch nary drap of the pizen stuff on this place."

The embodiment of the majesty of these United States now proceeded to prove himself a human being and a good sport. He could take a joke.

"That's all right, old man! The laugh is on me. If you'll find some more cups, we'll dispose of a gallon or so of the evidence, at the expense of the government; and I hope my friend here will be as lucky the next time!"

"They ain't goin' to be no next time," responded Amos dryly, as he climbed to his seat and clucked to his horses. "Reckon I'll have to be spuddin' along if I'm goin' to sell the balance of this here white mule!"

An hour later, having peddled his wares up and down Crockettsburg's narrow main street, Amos was preparing to set out for home.

"Don't look like I'd buy any purties fer the gal," he thought, as he counted the few one-dollar bills and the handful of "chicken feed" that he had realized from his day's work. "But if hit hadn't 'a' been fer her impidence I'd 'a' slep' to-night in a jail house! By gonnies, I'm goin' to git her somethin' if hit busts me!"

He had hitched his team behind the courthouse, and was walking down the street toward the Beehive, the chief emporium of the mountain metropolis. As he passed the Citizens' Bank, he was accosted by the vice president, cashier, assistant cashier, paying teller, receiving teller, and bookkeeper, all these officials being combined in the ample proportions of Milt Lovingood. Milt was in the act of locking the outside door preparatory to entering his flivver and going home for the day. Seeing Amos, however, he hailed the mountaineer familiarly.

"Hello there, Amos! You're just the man I'm looking for. I was going to write you a letter in the morning. Step inside a minute."

Amos, whose only connection with a bank had been when he had been compelled to pay Cam Brigg's twelve-hundred-dollar note, followed Lovingood with misgivings.

"Ye ain't wantin' me to pay off another note, air ye Milt?" he asked timorously.

"Well, not exactly that," the banker replied banteringly; "although it is in connection with that Briggs' note that I wanted to see you."

"I don't never want to hear that skunk's name agin," growled Amos sullenly. "He ruined me—ye know that."

"But, Amos, I rather thought you'd be glad to hear his name at least *once* more."

"What's he went an' done now? D'ye know whar he is? If ye do, I reckon I'll take my ol' rifle gun an' go polecat huntin'."

"That won't be necessary. Amos, I've got some good news for you. I had a letter to-day from Cam. He's been out in New Mexico, and he's either struck oil or got religion. I don't know which. Anyhow, he sent a draft to cover all the debts he left here. If you'll just sign these papers, I'll turn over your twelve hundred right now, with seventy-two dollars for a year's interest."

Amos Cagle's throat muscles were working strangely, and it was a full minute before he could speak. Then, with a voice as shaky as the huge fist that scrawled his signature, he gulped:

"Jes' put the twelve hundred on deposit, Milt, an' give me the seventy-two in cash money. I reckon ye'll think I've went crazy, but I'm goin' down to the Beehive an' buy that gal of mine the gol-durnedest, rip-snortin'est dress they've got in this dad-blamed town."

THE CURIN'EST REMEDY

In the open doorway of an indescribably tumble-down log cabin far up the slopes of Gregory Bald sat an elderly mountaineer, gaunt of frame and unkempt of attire. Abe Lincoln McTavish, known to the little world of Hoot Owl Cove as "Doc Link", was innocent of book learning and devoid of any license to practice the art of Æsculapius in the State of North Carolina, but the ailing and the "porely" of the cove folk sent for him, listened to his oracular pronouncements, and took his potions with wry faces but unwavering trust.

The "doctor" was putting the last touches of preparedness to his favorite and only surgical "instermint", with which he had lanced many a "bile, pone, or risin'", and had amputated sundry crushed fingers and toes with no anæsthetic save putting the luckless patient under the influence of his ponderous fist.

That surgical instrument was nothing more or less than his trusty Barlow knife, an ancient "frog-sticker" whose single blade tapered to a needlelike point. He was sharpening it carefully upon a whetstone kept well lubricated with "ambeer" from the juicy quid of home-cured twist he was chewing. The medical adviser of Hoot Owl paused as Harrison Brinkley's canvas-top wagon lumbered up the rocky road and stopped in front of the gate. Everybody who came by Doc Link's gate stopped.

"Howdy, doc! How's all?" Brinkley called from his seat under the wagon-bow.

" 'Bout as common, Harrison. Light an' blow yer hosses!"

"Can't, I reckon. Jes' been down on Bobcat to see the new sawmill. Hit's a main big outfit—double band an' resaw. They'll be workin' three hunderd hands in a month."

"Reckon they'll be buildin' a right smart settlemint on Bobcat," McTavish surmised.

"Yeah, hit's lookin' like a reg'lar town a'ready. Must be nigh a hunderd comp'ny houses strung up an' down the holler. They've got a new schoolhouse with a passel of fotch-on teachers, an' a horspittle, an' a comp'ny doctor."

At the mention of the doctor McTavish snorted with contempt. "Huh! Bet he's some young store-clo'es dude that's got a sheepskin from a college an' don't know nothin' exceptin' what he's read in a book!"

"I 'low ye're right, doc. I seed him to-day. He's shore young an' stylish lookin'."

"Well," the old man replied with evident complacency, "I ain't no man to brag, but I l'arnt doctorin' from an' ol' Injun an' I've follered hit fer over forty year. I've got it figgered out that the three best medicines that the Good Man ever made He put right here in these here mountains."

"What's them three, doc?" the admiring Brinkley inquired.

"Why, they's turpentime, balsam ile, an' corn liquor. The three will cure any sickness that ain't oncurable. But hit takes knowin' how to use 'em, an' right thar's whar I've got the advantage o' these here town doctors."

"Right ye air, doc!" agreed the wagoner with warmth. "I don't want no book doctor a-dosin' me ner mine. Doctorin's a gift, I say, which them that's got it don't need no schoolin', an' them that ain't, schoolin' wouldn't do 'em no good nohow!"

Having delivered himself of this bit of native wisdom, Brinkley clucked to his horses and the old mountain schooner quickly disappeared around a bend in the road. Abe Lincoln McTavish, however, despite his assumed air of complacent disdain, was inwardly disturbed. For three decades and more he had set his face resolutely against the subtle encroachments of new-fangled notions into the seventeenth-century world of Hoot Owl Cove. Once it had been the threat of the railroad that rumor said was about to penetrate the shut-in valley. Fortunately that menace to tranquillity had come no nearer than the forks of Bobcat Branch, some miles down the way, where the new sawmill had now come.

Lately there had been the invasion of the automobile, and despite his best efforts the impudent chug-chug of a laboring flivver could nowadays be occasionally heard churning through the mud and over the stones, startling the wild creatures of the far-flung forest. Doc McTavish had no use for "them steam buggies," and little patience with those hankerers after novelty who insisted on riding in them.

It had been likewise with the telephone, the tractor, the new-time schools, the changing modes of dress; and every insidious disguise under which the octopus of Modernism sought to thrust its tentacles into Hoot Owl Cove.

But this newest assault upon the citadel of things-as-they-used-to-be was the most sinister threat of all. It struck home—at his own door. Why, the whole countryside had looked to him to set its broken bones, to pull its aching molars, to relieve its "misery," and to cure its "dyspepsy," its "side pleurisy," and its "rheumatiz." When his crude pharmacopaia failed to accomplish the desired end, both physician and patient had always with commendable resignation attributed the grim outcome to the inscrutable workings of Providence, whose ways are past finding out.

Now, however, in the new and populous mill village he would have a formidable rival. He had heard enough of these educated doctors to know that they employed medicines and methods wholly foreign to his ken. And scorn and rage surged hot in the old hillsman's heart.

"I'll show 'im! Ey gonnies, I'll show 'im!" he muttered half aloud as he resumed the whetting of his "instermint".

Ordinarily the deep, crashing roar of the six-o'clock whistle at the big sawmill on Bobcat Branch startled Lois Pearson into bolt-upright, joyous awareness that a great new day had climbed the Gregory Bald and was peeping down upon the little white schoolhouse and its cozy teacherage. This morning, however, she slowly dragged herself to the threshold of consciousness only to meet at that doorway the unusual and unexpected sensations of pain and dizziness. It was queer, but it was real enough. Lois Pearson, first assistant in the brand-new school at Bobcat, was just too ill to get up. And for almost the first time in her young life, too.

Mrs. Dunn, housekeeper at the teachers' cottage, laid her large, motherly hands on the schoolma'am's throbbing temples. "No, Miss Pearson, ye mustn't try to git up. Ye can't teach no school to-day. An' ye ort to have a doctor." It took several minutes and a good deal of argument to get that through the young woman's pretty head, but she finally yielded to the housekeeper's insistence and consented to have the lumber company's physician, the only regular doctor within twenty miles, called in to see her. Mrs. Dunn dispatched a mountain boy to the mill superintendent's office to ask for Doctor Heywood. The lad returned presently with the air of one having done his full duty, or perhaps a trifle more than that.

"No'm, the new doc ain't thar to-day. He's away up at Camp Six whar they've had a wreck an' three men hurt. But I seed the *ol'* doc an' axed him to come, an' he'll be here d'reckly."

"But who is the old doctor?" queried Lois, who was still pretty much a stranger in the scattered settlement.

"Why, hit's Doc Link McTavish, ma'am," the housekeeper replied. "He's been our doctor here ever sinst I was a gal-like."

"Is he a competent physician?"

"Law yes, miss," Mrs. Dunn assured her. "Ever'body knows Doc Link an' most folks round here confidences him more'n they do this here young feller the comp'ny hired."

"Well, on your recommendation I'll have him come," Miss Pearson consented, being too miserable to argue much about anything.

"Howdy do, missy! How d'ye come on?"

Lois Pearson turned her aching head upon the pillow to look into the keen black eyes of a tall, awkward man dressed in a baggy suit of nondescript gray. He wore neither collar nor tie and his shaggy iron-gray hair was in need of both shears and comb. But the eyes had a friendly twinkle and the gruff voice was kindly.

"Is this Doctor McTavish?" the girl asked in surprise.

"Well, hit passes fer him," the gruff voice replied with a good-natured drawl. "An' what mought *your* name be?"

"I'm Miss Pearson, one of the teachers here," Lois answered, puzzled by the rude attire and ruder speech of the visitor. Still, she remembered, these country doctors sometimes affect a rustic manner that belies their professional skill.

"Have ye got a right smart o' misery? Whar do ye hurt the wust?"

Briefly Lois detailed her symptoms. "I think I must have a good deal of temperature," she concluded. "You'll want a glass of water to rinse your thermometer, won't you doctor?"

Doc McTavish, if the truth must be told, had never seen a clinical thermometer in his life. "No, ma'am, I don't need nary glass ner nary do-which-it to tell what's ailin' a body. They's no neecessity fer no wagonload o' tools ner no drugstore full o' fotchon medicine to cure folks if they've got the right doctor. Poke out yer tongue!"

The patient, too much astonished for words, obeyed. The doctor scrutinized the poked-out member gravely, uttering solemn "Hm's" at intervals.

"Ain't been much keen fer yer vittles fer a spell, eh?"

"No, doctor, I haven't had any appetite for a day or two."

Courtesy of the Great Smoky Mountains National Park   Photographed by Jim Shelton

A barracks at Camp 18 at Three Forks Prong - 1922.

"Let's count them pulse!"

The big, clumsy fingers closed upon the girl's wrist, while the doctor gazed at the dial of a small cabinet clock on the mantel. "Ye're right much upsot, missy. What ye been doin' to git this a way?"

"Well, I've worked hard to get the children started off well at school and I haven't had enough time for exercise."

"Yeah, I 'low ye've got werried a heap at the devilmint of them feisty younguns. This here school-teachin's a powerful confindin' job. Ye ort to be mighty keerful an' not strain yer mind. I've knowed of cases whar eddicated folks has plumb bodaciously busted their intelleck."

Lois Pearson began to see the light. She suddenly realized that she was being attended by one of the crudest of the old-time mountain doctors, a few of whose tribe still survive in the remoter nooks of Great Smoky. She hardly knew whether to be angry or amused, but quickly decided on the latter.

"Hit's a good thing ye sont fer me," the old hillsman went on. "I ain't no man to brag, but folks round here will tell ye I'm a sure-fire expert at curin' a'most any kind of sickness. I'll fix ye up a doste." And producing from his weather-worn saddlebags a flask containing a slightly amber liquid, he called to Mrs. Dunn to bring a spoon.

"Pardon me, doctor, but what is it you are planning to give me?" Lois inquired. She didn't want to hurt the old man's feelings, but she wasn't going to swallow just anything.

"Hit's somethin' these here town doctors knows mighty little about," McTavish replied with a pride that fairly shone in the face. "Hit's the curin'est medicine the Good Man ever made. Hit's balsam ile."

"Balsam oil? Why, I never heard of it before—at least as a medicine to be taken internally. Is it a cathartic?"

The man's expression was utterly blank for a moment, but he rallied heroically. "No ma'am, 'tain't nothin' like that. Hit's jes' what I told ye hit was—the curin'est medicine they is fer what's ailin' ye now. Here! Swaller hit down!"

But the schoolmistress of Bobcat, albeit she smiled most amiably, was resolute. "Thanks, doctor, but I've never taken any medicine except on the prescription of a regular practitioner. I was really expecting Doctor Heywood to see me, and I'll just wait until he can come." Perhaps she might have been a bit more diplomatic about it, but then she wasn't used to having doctors about. She realized instantly, however, that she had given mortal offense.

"All right, ma'am," the crestfallen McTavish replied in a tone that was meant to be crushingly polite. "Ye don't have to take hit less'n ye choose to. All I've got to say is, these here briggaty town doctors, with their dude clo'es an' their fancy contraptions, is a-killin' a sight of people. Everwhen ye git to dostin' up on them pizen pills this here young whippersnapper of a sawmill doctor gives, ye're like as not to wake up a-layin' in yer coffin! Good day to ye—I've done told ye!" And in superb dudgeon the "balsam doctor" strode out of the room.

Next morning Miss Pearson was somewhat better, but at Mrs. Dunn's insistence she repeated her call for the company physician. When Doctor Heywood arrived, as trim and immaculate as if his practice were in the exclusive residence section of a big city instead of in a straggling lumber camp in the mountains, he found a most winsome patient propped up on the pillows, over which her chestnut hair lay in a luxurious mass.

In the course of his busy rounds he had caught occasional long-range glimpses of the first-assistant "lady teacher," but not until now had he realized how different she was from the typical country schoolmarm he had pictured her to be. He laughed with her over her account of the native doctor's visit, but when he spoke his tone was serious.

"Unfortunately the old codger can't be taken merely as a joke," he said. "He is causing me no end of annoyance and trouble. Many of the people in the cove swallow his worthless dope and his equally worthless advice wholesale. He pooh-poohs every sanitary measure I try to introduce, and sneaks around the neighborhood ridiculing me and substituting his balsam oil and corn whisky for the drugs I prescribe."

"Then his precious 'ile' is really worthless?"

"Why, practically so, yes. It might have a slight antiseptic value if it were clean. Otherwise it has no medicinal quality to speak of."

"Well, I fear I made a mortal enemy of him yesterday when I refused to take his oil and told him I wanted you to see me."

"Yes, I dare say you did. And it isn't at all improbable that you'll hear from him in more ways than one. He's a crafty old faker, and we may both have occasion to know him better in the future."

Then Doctor Heywood, leaving a prescription and nodding a cheery farewell, took his leave. It wouldn't be quite fair to him to hint that down in his heart he wished his charming patient might soon again be ill enough to necessitate a second professional call. Of course he didn't wish just that—but he did resolve that he would pay some nonprofessional post-convalescence calls. And he did.

Within a fortnight both the young doctor and the schoolmistress had occasion to recall the incident of the dismissal of Doc Link McTavish. Evidently the iron had struck deep into the old man's soul. The story of the indignity he had suffered at the hands of the "furrin' teacher lady" had been "norated" up and down the hollows and had grown with each recital.

"She as good as tol' me I weren't no reg-lar doctor. She wouldn't tetch what I give her an' she purt' nigh busted out laffin' right in my face." This, in substance, was the burden of the jilted one's original lament, but by the time it was bruited about for a week it was being indignantly told that "this here uppity furrin' woman jes' p'intedly ordered Doc Link out o' the house like a yaller dawg an' said she wouldn't let him doctor a sick hoss or a cow-brute of hern. Then she told him she was expectin' that nice, smart, purty-lookin' young doctor an' she jes' knowed he'd cure her in a minute! Haw! Haw! Haw!"

So the gossips' tongues had wagged, and even the mountain children, quick to echo in word and act the tone of the fireside chatter, were finding annoying little ways to express their hostility. Ignore it as she might, Lois Pearson was fully aware that her social status in the narrow little world of lumber stacks and whining saws and pine-box shanties had suffered a change for the worse.

As for the company doctor, he bore the heavier brunt of the old man's odium. He had worked for weeks to introduce a few first principles of sanitation into the camp. At his suggestion the mill officials had furnished door and window screens for all the houses of the employees. Many of these, however, were left lying unused or were converted into ash sifters, squirrel cages, or chicken coops.

"Doc Link 'lowed hit was jist a fool idy that flies makes sickness. He says the Bible talks about flies but hit don't say nary word about germs!"

Later the company ordered the vaccination of the whole camp and inoculation against typhoid and diphtheria. The teachers in the school urged the children to avail themselves of this free protection. But a storm of protest burst upon the head of both physician and teachers.

"Doc Link says this here vaccination is a pack of foolishness. He says more folks has lost their arms from vaccination than smallpox ever killed. He says wearin' a lump of asafidity round yer neck an' takin' a little balsam ile ever'day will keep off might' nigh any sickness."

So the children were in open rebellion and played truant for days at a time. One burly mill hand sat in his open doorway with a double-barreled shotgun across his knees and dared the world to try to vaccinate him or hisn. Doc Link was making good his threat to "*show* that thar town doctor."

Winter came early and was unusually severe. The top of old Gregory Bald glistened with snowcaps almost continuously from Thanksgiving until late January. Soon after Christmas the epidemic of influenza that was sweeping the whole country invaded the shut-in world of Hoot-Owl-on-the-Bobcat. The mysterious plague was recognized at once by Heywood, but most of the cove folk refused to be told that it was anything but the usual "colds" with which most mountaineers sniffle resignedly the whole winter long.

Among the mill hands, however, scores of cases quickly developed and there were frequent complications and a few deaths. The epidemic soon assumed proportions truly alarming. The big sawmill was operating with only a bare third of its employees. The office force on some days was reduced to a timekeeper and two or three overworked clerks.

The school was closed and the schoolhouse converted into an emergency hospital, the regular infirmary being taxed far beyond its capacity. The company officials wired for cots and supplies. Lois Pearson and the other teachers, having become volunteer nurses, came and went among the sick, taking temperatures, recording symptoms, and administering the doctor's medicines according to his instructions.

Doctor Heywood was going day and night. Many trips he made on foot to out-of-the-way nooks among the gloomy hills where no car, nor even a horse and buggy, could go. Over lonely trails he struggled by lantern light to find some lost cabin where a stricken family of perhaps a dozen was left to the crude nursing of a half-grown boy or girl. The physician's skill was matched single-handed against the pestilence that walked in darkness—and against the incredible childishness of the illiterate people.

Most discouraging of all was the secret, subtle antagonism of the balsam doctor. Time after time when Heywood entered some lowly room where life

Courtesy of the Great Smoky Mountains National Park   Photographed by Edouard E. Exline

A demonstration moonshine whiskey still at the Camp Morgan CCC camp - 1935.

grappled with death he found that the old charlatan had been there before him, administering his "ile" and rotten liquor and sowing seeds of distrust and hostility against scientific treatment.

Sometimes when in desperation the panic-stricken family would at last call in the young doctor they would confide to him the reason why the call had come so late—often too late. "Doc Link argyed we ortn't to send fer ye. He says, 'That feller's killin' more'n he's curin'. If you-uns wants to git well ye jes' stick to balsam ile an' good liquor.'"

It was much the same at the improvised hospital where Lois Pearson was on duty sixteen hours a day. Not infrequently a patient would put up a pathetic plea. "I ain't used to these here new ways. I'm skeered to take these quare-lookin' powders an' sich. I wisht ye'd send fer Doc Link."

More than once a nurse would detect a suspicious odor around a bed and a search would disclose a flask of moonshine whisky or a bottle of balsam that had been surreptitiously brought in by a member of the patients household. Over the whole valley brooded a sinister suspicion against "furriners" in general and the "young doc" and the "teacher woman" in particular. And back of it all, as they well knew, was the malevolent cunning and the unsleeping jealousy of the balsam doctor.

One dark evening, when the epidemic was at its peak, Doctor Heywood and Lois Pearson were sitting in the office of the emergency hospital. The doctor, dog-tired after a hectic day, was looking over the nurses' charts and penciling brief memoranda of instructions for the night. There was a vigorous pounding at the front door. Mrs. Dunn answered the knock and ushered in a ragged mountain boy who shuffled awkwardly from one foot to another before he found his voice.

"Air you the comp'ny doctor?" he asked finally.

"Yes, sonny. What's on your mind?"

"I'm Carse Tucker from up at the head of Hoot Owl, right ferninst the Gap," he drawled. "Doc Link McTavish wants ye right off."

"Wants *me*?" Heywood asked in surprise. "There must be some mistake."

"Reckon not," the boy persisted. "Doc said he didn't know whether ye'd come or not, but he was powerful sot on havin' ye."

For an instant Heywood was suspicious. "What's the matter, sonny?" he queried again. "I can't understand why he should be wanting me."

"Well, ye see, doc's grandson, 'Little' Linky, has got some quare sickness. He's turrible bad off."

"Isn't the old man attending him?"

"Yeah, he's been doctorin' him fer a week, but he's skeered the little feller's goin' to die on him. Ye see the kid's named fer his grandsire an' the ol' man's a plumb fool about him. That's fer why he wants ye to come. He said hit was awful urgin'."

Heywood's decision was made in a flash. "Well, sonny, we have our hands full here, but if the old man really wants help I'll come. Are we ready, Miss Pearson?"

"*We*?" Lois asked in surprise as the lad shuffled out of the room.

"Yes, *we*. I shall need a nurse on this case, I'm sure. Get your things ready, please."

The doctor's roadster roared and pounded through the night, up the steep, rocky road that had been made for oxen and sleds. As he rounded a sharp turn near the Gap he saw the gaunt figure of McTavish standing in the road in front of his cabin. His excited gestures bespoke his agitation. Stark fear was written in every line of his haggard face.

"Doc," he began before Heywood could get out of the car, "my grandbaby's got a master bad sickness. His paw an' maw has done give him up. My treatment ain't workin' like hit ginerally does. Of course, I reckon ye know I've said some purty mean things about ye an'--"

"Let that pass, old man," Heywood broke in. "Let's have a look at the boy."

Then McTavish caught sight of Miss Pearson, who had stepped out of the car dressed in the costume of a nurse. Recognizing her instantly as the patient who had refused his treatment and dismissed him in favor of his rival, he bristled up for a moment, with a curt "Howdy, miss!" But the fight was out of him now. The sense of his utter helplessness in the face of the unseen enemy that was stalking his own threshold had made him lamblike.

"I'm proud ye come, missy. I need ye both. I've done my best an' I don't know nary nuther thing to do. I want you an' the young doc to fight as ye never fit before!"

The sick boy lay on a rough straw bed, his only covering a much-faded and soiled quilt of quaint mountain design. The room, with doors and windows tightly closed, reeked with the blended odors of turpentine, balsam and whisky. The lad was in a stupor—had lain so for hours, the grandfather explained, save when roused to have more whisky poured down his throat. He moaned at intervals and his labored breathing could be heard even in the next room.

Seated round the fireplace where a log fire threw its fitful glare into the room, huddled a dozen or more neighbors, waiting in stolid silence to see whether it was to be life or death for the stricken boy. The men chewed or smoked. Some of the women vigorously plied the "toothbresh," or snuff stick.

Near the bedside the boy's mother, distraught with grief and fear, rocked back and forth in her chair lamenting loudly. "Oh, Lordy, Lordy, Linky! I cain't bear to see ye go! Oh, Lordy, whatever will I do when ye're gone?" The father, a younger edition of the balsam doctor, tried in vain to quiet his wife. "Don't take on so, Jinny! Maybe ol' pappy an' the young doc'll pull him through."

"Get everybody out of the room and open a window!" was Heywood's first order, spoken quietly to Miss Pearson. He opened his medicine case, took the boy's temperature, timed his pulse and respiration and made a thorough stethoscopic examination of the chest. The grandfather remained by the bedside, watching every movement, scanning the younger man's face by the light of the flickering kerosene lamp.

"What ails him, doc? Hit ain't like no sickness ever I seed."

"A bad case of pneumonia," Heywood replied briefly. "Much congestion in both lungs, though more involvement in the left. The temperature is typical and the heart seems strong and steady. I should say it is now about the crisis of the case, and it is simply a matter of how good a fight the lad can put up. We must give him every chance."

"Don't ye want to give him some more liquor, doc? Hit's a cold night outside an' he ort to be kep' warm."

"Not a drop!" Heywood retorted brusquely. "He's poisoned with alcohol already. Please understand, old man, that if I'm to undertake this case my orders are to be obeyed to the letter. I'm not promising anything, mind you, but the boy has a chance and I'm going to see that he gets it. You've got to help by doing what I say."

The neighbors left after a while though with evident resentment at the refusal of their well-intentioned offers to "set up" all night with the sick boy. The rest of the household, at Miss Pearson's insistence, went to bed in the back room. The children lay on pallets on the floor, their feet forming a semicircle round the fire on the hearth.

Heywood and Lois stayed all night, the doctor watching closely the changing symptoms as the sick boy in the darkness of delirium battled for breath and life. McTavish sat with them, though he had not lain down for two nights. He hung on every motion of physician and nurse, following pathetically when Lois would step out of the room to bring a spoon or a glass of water.

Once, long after midnight they motioned to him to remain on guard while they went out of doors "for a breath of fresh air." They stood together for some time on the little portico of the cabin. The crisp, moonless night was uncannily still. The lonely house on the mountainside seemed to stand on an infinitesimal island in a boundless ocean of darkness and nothingness. Only the soft stir of the wind in the spruce broke the utter silence.

What the doctor and the nurse were talking about as they murmured in a semiwhisper isn't really a part of this story; but they seemed to find it absorbing enough. At any rate their "breath of fresh air" seemed to involve a good many respirations, not to speak of an occasional sigh and a little gasp or two.

Suddenly from far in the valley below came the faint baying of a hound at some distant neighbor's cabin. Instantly two gaunt bear-dogs stirred uneasily beneath the porch floor and set up deep-throated answering howls, so weird and dismal that they made the girl's blood run cold. That was the reason, no doubt, why she impulsively seized the doctor's arm in the darkness and why that arm was thrown protectingly about her shoulders.

Before they could turn to go inside to see whether the patient had been aroused by the commotion without, the door behind them was flung open and the grandfather stood cowering there, the pallor of his face made ghastly by the yellow lamplight.

"Oh, my God, folks!" he moaned. "That thar was a sign—them dawgs a-howlin' that a way. Linky's goin' to die! I was lookin' fer it all the time, an' now hit's shore an' certain!"

Almost fiercely Heywood motioned him into silence. "Now, see here, old man, you've got too much sense to believe in signs like that! Let me show you some *real* signs."

He took up the chart the nurse had kept hourly through the night. "See here! The boy's temperature is slowly subsiding—a whole degree lower now than at dark. His respiration is slower and easier and his pulse better. I think we can say that he is safely passing the crisis."

"I shore hope to God ye're right, doc," was the fervent response. "But how ye can tell so much by them thar little glass tricks an' that rubber tiliphone of a thing ye listen through, I can't figger out. An' they's so many onexplainable things happens in these dark mountains that we folks that's lived here so long jes' can't help believin' in signs."

Daylight came at last, and after the night's vigil the watchers were able to assure the anxious parents and the grandsire that the boy had taken a definite turn for the better. "He's still a very sick lad, of course," Heywood explained, "and he will require the most careful nursing for several days. I'm leaving Miss Pearson here for the present, and you must do just as she directs."

McTavish stood watching the doctor as he gave the patient a final examination. The look in his face was one of wordless admiration, almost of awe. And when Heywood rose to go, the crust of the old man's stoicism, which sixty years of mountain life had hardened into stone, broke like a shattered jar and his pent-up emotion gushed forth in a flood.

"Glory Halleluyer, doc! You an' the little lady has fit it out with Death an' ye've whupped him to a fare-ye-well! I ain't done neither one of ye right, but hit was jist because I'm a ol' ignor'nt, ornery mountain boomer that didn't know no better. From now on if ary man, woman, or youngun in Hoot Owl or on Bobcat ever opens their head to say one little word again' ye, I aim to p'intedly frale hell out of 'em, so help me Joab!"

Then the three of them walked down to the gate, and the balsam doctor, awkwardly slipping a flash of the fragrant "ile" into Heywood's hand, stammered his gratitude.

"You young folks must excuse a ol' fool like me, but I seed las' night how things was betwixt ye. Jes' take this here along. Hit ain't no 'count fer pneumony fever, but hit shore is the curin'est remedy fer colic an' croup! And you-all may be needn't it one o' these days."

"VENGENANCE IS MINE"

The red ball of the sun dropped into a seething cauldron of foamy clouds behind the summit of the Great Bald. In the doorway of an ancient log house by the side of the stony road that wound upward toward the Gap, sat Granny Mag Tollett. In the room behind her a girl of eighteen or thereabout, straight, deep-chested, and comely, hummed a plaintive ballad as she washed the supper dishes. "Them yaller clouds forebodes fallin' weather, Dilsie," mumbled the grandmother, as a fitful gust rattled the festoons of dry bean pods swung from the porch rafters.

"Yes, Granny," replied the girl, coming to the door. "I've been listenin' to the wind a-roarin' like the big waters in the balsams up yander t'wards the Chimneys. Hit's drappin' down now into the spruce."

Her dishwashing finished, Dilsie Tollett drew her chair to the porch beside that of her grandmother. The two sat for a time in silence, gazing out across the undulating ridges toward the fiery sunset. Truth to tell, though, it was not the riotous glory of the dying day, nor the placid beauty of the tinted ridge-tops, that had drawn Mag Tollett to her accustomed seat in the door of the ancestral cabin. This evening, as always at the close of a summer day, her gaze roamed no farther than a low, grass-grown knoll rising out of the little meadow across the road.

Crowning the knoll, and silhouetted against the flaming western skyline, stood a rudely-carved slab of brownish stone within a tiny, picketed enclosure. The pickets were a dingy yellow with forgotten whitewash, and were interlaced with wild honeysuckle. The slab, which marked the head of a vine-tangled grave, was no longer upright, but tilted at a crazy angle. "I'm afeared yer pappy's tomb rock's goin' to blow clear down in the fust big wind, Honey," quavered the old woman. "I've been layin' off fer me an' you to git out thar an' h'ist it up."

"I'll help ye evern'n ye say, but Granny, I wis't we cauld sell a calf or somethin' an' put up a boughten stone in place of that homemade one," replied the girl wistfully.

"Looky here, Missy," retorted the grandmother tartly, "whatever put sich a crazy idy in yer head? Didn't I take the hoss an' sled that rock down from the qu'rry? Didn't I fashion it with yer grandsir's cold chisel an' carve the writin' on it with my own hand?"

"Sure, Granny, I know that, but hit gives me the creeps to set here ever' night an' look at them words on it."

"What's the matter with them words, Gal? Ain't they the truth, the whole truth, an' nothin' but the truth? 'Here lies Tom Tollett, on the spot wher he were murdered by Devil John Cutshaw.' Ain't that the God's truth?"

"Yes, Granny, hit's the truth, I know, but what's the good of puttin' it whar we've got to keep thinkin' of it all our days. Pappy's dead an' gone, an' John Cutshaw's been in the pen for five years now."

"Child, I want ye should think about it all yer days! Ye're all the child Tommy had, an' yer mammy died the night ye was borned. When he was shot down right thar in the medder, I tuck ye to raise. Then I put up that monument stone an' gravened it thataway so's ye couldn't never fergit!"

The girl made no reply. The years of stern tutelage in the lonely cabin had taught her the dumb submission that is the highest virtue of childhood in the mountains.

Mag Tollett presently turned to her granddaughter. "Honey, fetch the lantern an' let's bright up the globe while we're settin'. The big meetin' commences tomorrer night an' hit's the dark of the moon."

Dilsie obeyed with alacrity. "I'm glad they'll be somethin' to do," she volunteered with a glimmer of interest. "Hit won't be so lonesome-like."

Mag set to work polishing the smoky globe, alternately filming it with her breath and rubbing it with a cotton rag.

Suddenly Dilsie stepped to the edge of the porch and leaned against the rustic handrail. "Listen, Granny! They's somebody ridin' up thisaway! I heared hosses' hoofs on the rocks."

"Some feller over on Turkeytail goin' the nigh way through the Gap, I reckon," surmised Mag.

In a few minutes a horseman came into view. He drew rein at the gate.

"Why hit's Mosey Riddle, Granny!" Dilsie whispered as her young eyes recognized the rider.

"Howdy, Folkses!" came a neighborly greeting out of the dusk.

"Tol'able, Mosey, how's yerself? Light an' come in," responded the old woman without rising.

"No, Ma'am, much obleeged. I jes rid by to ax ye heard the news."

"What news?" inquired both women at once.

"John Cutshaw's out!"

"Oh, goodness, no, Mosey! Ye know he ain't!" shouted Mag. The girl barely rescued the globe of the lantern as it rolled out of the old woman's nerveless fingers.

"Yes, Mis' Tollett, hit's so. I got it straight from Lawyer Benson in town this mornin'."

"But, Mosey, he was sent up fer life, an' hit hain't been but five year next month."

"Anyhow, he's out," repeated Mosey. "The Guvnor signed his pardon Tuesday, an' they say he's headed fer home. I knowed you-uns wouldn't like to hear it, but I thought ye ort to know. Well, I'll be pluggin' along. Looks like it's goin' to storm some."

Stunned by the tidings, the women sat in wordless consternation for a time. Mag shook her head at intervals in mingled doubt and dismay. "Dilsie," she said presently, "I'd rather than a million dollars this wouldn't 'a' been! They'll be trouble on Thunderin' Creek 'count of this! I can't figger out, though, how any guvnor would turn loose a man like that."

"John Cutshaw's got rich kin out in the flat country, Granny. They ain't hardly nothin' folks can't do if they've got money," replied the girl, with the dull pessimism of youth that has lived in the shadow of querulous age.

"Listen, Dilsie!" There was a ring of decision in the cracked voice. "Run an' git the ol' huntin' horn, the one yer grandsir used to b'ar-hunt with."

Dilsie returned in a moment with a great brass-lipped oxhorn of remarkable length and size. The grandmother put it to her shrunken mouth, but only a squawky wheeze issued forth. "Here, you take it, Honey! Ye're big an' stout in yer chist. Blow four long toots like ye was callin' in the b'ar dawgs; then wait a minute an' blow four more. Do it three times thataway."

The young girl obeyed, putting her full strength into deep-throated blasts that shrilled down the valley in the dusk. Above the roar of the wind in the pines, the echoes floated back, wave on wave. It was the pibroch. So did the highland clansmen sound the battle cry and the council call down the wooded glens of Scotland in the old days! So have the mothers of mountain men, time out of mind, sent forth summons and warnings to their imperiled sons!

"That'll fetch 'em!" declared Mag, as the reverberations died away. "The boys will be comin' in a hurry, hearin' their pappy's ol' huntin' horn. Hit hain't been blowed since't the day John Cutshaw killed yer paw."

The lurid twilight faded swiftly into the darkness of a moonless night. An hour after the great horn had sounded, the gaunt hound that lay at Mag Tollett's feet stirred uneasily, slunk down to the gate, and sent up a long-drawn howl that silenced the calls of the whippoorwills for a space. In a moment an answering note came up from far below. "Uncle Zeb's comin', Granny! That's his Gyp answerin' ol' Duke. I know that dawg's voice same as a human's!"

"Zeb would come past Cort's an' Rudy's an' fetch them," soliloquized Mag. "Jimmy'll git here as soon as the balance of 'em, even if he does have to come a mile farther. My baby'll ride hard when he hears his mammy a-callin'!"

Sure enough in a few minutes four lank horsemen were dismounting at the gate amid much nickering of horses and yapping of hounds. The pibroch had brought them all, the four sturdy hillsmen who owned most of the Thundering Creek valley, and dominated all of it. Each ruled his own household with a hand of iron, according to the code of the mountains, but he knew naught else than to "mind Maw" as implicitly in manhood as he had done when the maternal "hickory" had been more wholesomely feared than the paternal thrashings. "Here we air, Maw. What's happened?" called Zeb, the oldest, as he looped his bridle rein over the gatepost.

"Plenty's happened," replied the mother laconically, as the sons filed into the house. "I don't like to tell ye, but ye've got to know. The guvnor's pardoned John Cutshaw, an' he's comin' back here, tomorrer like as not."

A low growl of rage rumbled in the shadowy room, like the first far organ tones of thunder. "I knowed they was trouble when I heard paw's ol' horn," muttered Zeb. "Never expected, though, nothin' like this!"

"I've got jest one say about it," remarked the quiet-voiced Rudy, with ominous calm. "If the law can't keep him out of this cove, I've got somethin' that can!" His right hand moved across his body to rest eloquently upon the handle of a huge pistol.

"Rudy, ye're talkin' sense!" exclaimed Red Jim, the youngest of the four. He was the fire eater of the Tollett clan. "If we'd 'a' had the speerit an' spunk we'd ought to, John Cutshaw would 'a' been put whar no guvnor on earth could 'a' turned him out! I told ye back thar lettin' rattlesnakes an' Cutshaws live was bad business!"

"Hit's the livin' gospel, Jimmy," echoed Cort; "we was lookin' to the law an' the govermint fer justice, an' they've done us dirt! If you-uns will stand by me, we'll put the scoundrel in a heap tighter an' darker place than them state convict mines afore Saturday night!"

"I'll stand by ye till the end," vowed Red Jim fervently. "If the court can't give no satisfaction fer Tom's killin', his blood brothers will git satisfaction!"

"Here, you boys!" Mag Tollett's thin voice rang sharply. "Shet up, ever' one of ye. Ye're barkin' an' snappin' like a passel of wolves."

"Now, Maw," protested Red Jim hotly, "ye sot down on us a-doin' anything five years ago. We can't jist set still an' let that scoundrel strut up an' down this holler like he owned it! You know the Cutshaw tribes, the biggitiest cattle that ever was!"

"Now you-uns quit yer jawin', an' listen!" The mother's eyes flashed, and her words cracked like a whip. "Ye don't none of ye feel worse toward John than I do! I've purt' nigh prayed my God to let me see that man layin' cold an' dead with a bullet through his heart! But I know, an' you know, that ain't right. Ye ain't goin' to do no killin'!"

"But, Maw," remonstrated Zeb, "that's what ye said before, an' look whar hit's got us! Thunderin' Creek ain't a safe place fer nobody with him a-roamin' loose!"

"Now don't give yer mammy none of yer back-talk, Zebby. I know as well as you that riddin' this cove of that pizin reptile would make ever'body on

Thunderin' Creek draw their breath easier; but you boys ain't goin' to do it! No Tollett's got blood on his hands, an' ye ain't goin' to stain 'em now. That's all they is to it!"

The council was ended. For the present, at least, save for black looks and muffled threats, the desperate rage of the brothers had spent itself. Mag Tollett's boys would mind their mother. "The thing fer all of ye to do," she counseled, as the four untied their mounts at parting, "is to 'tend to yer own business an' keep from crossin' that man's path all ye can. Me an' Dilsie aims to go reg'lar to the pertracted meetin', an' I'd be proud if you-uns would come. I'd like to see all of ye perfessers afore I'm called."

The Reverend Gabe Mumpower, an ungainly giant with a voice like thunder, sat hunched on a low wooden chair behind the rude pulpit in the Hardshell meetinghouse. His long legs were drawn up like a half-opened jackknife, while on his knees lay an open Bible. He thumbed the pages back and forth, a black frown lowering on his massive face. He was in the throes of thought, casting about for a text.

The mountain preacher glanced up as the door opened. Mag Tollett and Dilsie entered to take their accustomed seats. Behind them, with a certain awkward hesitance, four men in heavy boots entered noisily. The congregation looked around with mild surprise. The Tollett boys had not darkened a church door since anybody could remember.

The "singin' chor" was discoursing lugubrious minor strains, adjuring the luckless sinner to make ready for the lurid dawning of the Judgment Day. Outside the air was heavy, surcharged with gathering tempest. Granny Mag's falling weather was at hand. Occasional lightning flashes filled the room with dazzling whiteness after which the tiny oil lamps in their wall brackets glowed sickly yellow again.

The preacher apparently sensed a connection between the unexpected entrance of the Tollett men and the

Courtesy of the Great Smoky Mountains National Park Photographed by Edouard E. Exline

The hopper of Jim Carr's Tub Mill on the Little Pigeon River.

release of John Cutshaw, which had been "norated" far and wide and had set every tongue on Thundering Creek wagging. At any rate he began anew his search for a text, and soon settled back with the air of one who has found that for which he was looking.

When the "singin' chor" had scattered to their seats, the gaunt frame of Gabe Mumpower loomed aloft, his powerful shoulders humped above the reading desk. A sonorous bass voice droned the chosen scripture: "'Vengeance is mine; I will repay, saith the Lord!'"

"They's folks in this house tonight," the preacher began with startling abruptness, "that's got their good reasons fer cravin' vengeance. That's human nacher, an' they's a heap of it in us mountain folks."

Not one of the Tolletts so much as flickered an eyelash; yet something told Gabe Mumpower that his arrow had gone home. He began to "warm up," working gradually into his "weavin' way," as the mountain folk call the characteristic sway and swing of the backwoods preacher.

"But here's the Good Book a-talkin' tonight, a-talkin' louder than the wind a-roaring' out yander an' the thunder a-poppin'. What is it a-sayin'? Listen at it!" There were uneasy stirrings here and there. Gabe Mumpower had an uncomfortable way of growing personal in his sermons.

"Hit says, 'Mosey Riddle, this means you! Air ye holdin' a ol' grudge agin anybody, say that man that sot fire to yer barn an' burnt up yer craps an' them two purty sorrel hosses ye thought so much of? You've got to stop yer hatin', Mosey! Vengeance is mine!'"

"Listen agin! Hit says, 'Aunt Viny Dugger, do ye keep a-thinkin' all the time about that slick scamp that swindled ye out of the money ye'd saved fer yer old age? Git all that pizen out of yer heart. Vengeance is mine!'"

Mosey and Aunt Viny, both pillars in Zion, nodded soberly. The wrongs they had suffered were familiar history at every fireside in the valley. The booming voice rolled on.

"Hit says again, 'Grandmaw Tollett, you've had more to bear than most anybody! You've heard the blood of yer first-born callin' from the ground, an' God A'mighty knows how loud hit calls! But these here words was meant fer you too, an' yer boys thar! Vengeance is mine! says the Lord!'"

Under the harrowing directness of the relentless preacher, punctuated by the increasing tumult of the descending storm, Dilsie shuddered and wept audibly. The Tollett men kept their stolid composure. The aged mother's outward calm was as unbroken as their own.

Something cracked in the distance. It was too short and sharp for thunder. Mountain men have keen ears for sounds like that. It came again, nearer, nearer. No mistake this time! Any man in the room could tell what that sound was, even the caliber of the pistol that made it! Once more it dinned, six rapid shots, followed by rolling echoes; then came the clatter of hoofs on the stones. Round the bend of the road dashed a dozen hard-ridden horses pounding through the darkness.

An instant before they passed from view, a sheet of flame from the low-hanging clouds illumined the landscape like blazing noonday. In that fraction of a second Zeb and Red Jim Tollett, from their seat by a window, saw and recognized a large piebald horse that headed the procession. It was "Calico Dick," known everywhere on Thundering Creek as the favorite mount of Barry Cutshaw, brother of John, and present leader of the notorious clan. John himself they could not make out for certain. Both the Tolletts, however, noted a bent, heavily-blanketed rider in the center of the troop, apparently being supported by the arm of a horseman on either side.

Obviously the ex-convict's kinsman and cronies had gone to meet him at the distant railway station and had formed a rollicking bodyguard for his return to the hills. They had even dared to route his triumphal march past the Thundering Creek meetinghouse, the center of the Tollett settlement, and the very scene of his dastardly crime.

The sheer insolence of their daring fairly staggered the assembled crowd, and all but broke up the meeting. This was no minor breach of the mountaineer's unwritten code, to "shoot up" a peaceful settlement. To go whooping and shouting past a lighted church in a rival neighborhood has but one meaning, an insult and a taunt. For the Cutshaws to do it! Why, the very sight of a Cutshaw on Thundering Creek made a Tollett's jaw stiffen, and his eye glint cold as steel!

Involuntarily the Tolletts had leaped to their feet. The impetuous Red Jim had jumped up and started to raise the window at his side. A bench was overturned, and the noise frightened a dozen women and children into an outcry of terror.

The bellowing bass of the preacher roared above the tumult without and the confusion within. His long arms swung like threshing flails. "Set down thar, you Men! This is God A'mighty's house, an' ye dassent profane it with yer strife! The next lightnin' bolt may bust this meetin' house into a million splinters! Hit's a awful thing to trifle with God!"

The Tolletts stood sullenly in the aisle. If they had heard the stinging rebuke from the pulpit, they showed no sign of heeding it. Zeb made a movement toward the door. Mag Tollett's cracked voice rang out: "Zeb! Jimmy! All of ye, set down! If ye hain't got no respect fer the preacher nor no fear of the Lord, ye've sure got to mind yer maw! Set down, I say!"

Sulkily the big men faced about and took their seats. With the strangely effective art of the native orator, the mountain preacher proceeded to retake the lost ground. He paced up and down the platform beating the air with fists like hickory mauls. The roar of the storm was drowned by the torrent of impassioned eloquence within. The "big meetin'" on Thundering Creek had opened auspiciously.

Next day rumor sped on swift wings. Up and down the cove the story of the vaunting ride of the Cutshaws was noised about. At Beckley's corn mill, where the patrons were all Tolletts, Tollett kin, or Tollett sympathizers, the talk was free and vehement. "Hit's a plumb outrage!" declared Grannison Beckley, the miller, to each newcomer. "Them Tollett boys has tuck a heap. They kep' hands off an' let the law handle John when a lot of folks would 'a' saved the state the costivity of tryin' that feller, an' then feedin' an' clothin' him."

"That's gospel, Grannison!" was the usual reply. "But atter the way him an' his gang done last night, nobody couldn't blame the boys fer gittin' him."

Toward noon Mosey Riddle came with a sack of corn. Mosey was a loyal Tollett supporter, but he lived at the very edge of the Cutshaw settlement up the creek.

"Seed any signs of John Cutshaw today, Mosey?" inquired Beckley with eager curiosity.

"Hain't saw hair nor hide of him," replied Riddle. "However, I heared a right smart from Colfax Gudger. He's a renter on Barry Cutshaw's place an' lives not fur from me."

"What did he say?"

"Why, he says John come home sick, powerful sick, he 'lowed. Barry told Colfax that was why the guvnor pardoned him, 'cause he was might' nigh gone with the consumption. Said he tuck it in the mines."

"Pooh! That's jest a Cutshaw lie!" commented the miller scornfully. "The way he came a-tearin' through here last night don't fit in with no sich a tale as that!"

"I'm jest tellin' ye the way Colfax told me," continued Mosey. "He says they had to purt' nigh tote John from the deepo an' hold him on his hoss, he was that weak. Says they put him to bed right off, an' he ain't likely to ever git out of it."

Before the day was over, others had corroborated Riddle's report. John Cutshaw had been sent home from the state convict mines to die in his native mountains.

When Mag Tollett heard it, she answered not a word. Coming to the cabin door, she stood for a space gazing toward the familiar skyline. Finally her eyes moved back, and she looked at the tilted slab on top of the grassy knoll. "'Hit air app'inted to men once't to die, an' atter that the Jedgement,'" she quoted gloomily. "Hit don't seem hardly right fer him to die peaceable in a bed," she added after another brooding silence. "'Twont be so hard, though, to hold back the boys now. I've been skeered they'd run afoul of him some'rs."

For two weeks the "big meetin'" had punctuated the monotony of life on Thundering Creek with commas of diversion, dashes of novelty, and exclamation points of excitement. Preacher Gabe Mumpower had flung his thunderbolts with deadly aim and gloating zeal, to the delight of saints and the discomfiture of sinners. The crowds had increased steadily, but there had been a conspicuous dearth of "perfessions." This had become a matter of comment. "Somethin' quare about it," observed Mosey Riddle sagely at Beckley's mill one afternoon. "Preacher Gabe's sure brandishin' the swoard as valiant as ever I seed it, an' they's a good crap of mourners ever' night, but none of 'em don't come through. Jedgmatically they's somethin' back of it. I ain't talkin', but I've got my idies about it."

"They must be a Achan in the camp of Izrul, eh?" suggested Grannison Beckley quizzically.

"Ye're hittin' close, Grannison. I ain't callin' no names, but ol' Satan must 'a' had a hand in it, bringin' a certain feller back here jest in time to stir up strife endurin' the meetin'."

"Mought be, Mosey. The ol' boy's up to sich doin's!"

To Mag Tollett, however, there was not the slightest room for surprise. Preacher Gabe had tramped up to her cabin one afternoon to talk conditions over. Her piety and zeal were famous in the annals of the mountains. He found the truculent old woman sitting on her porch with her Bible in her lap. "Sister Tollett," he began, "if ever'body was a-ponderin' the Book thataway, they'd be souls a-bornin' ever' night. But they's somethin' wrong. I'm sore perplexed an' worried."

"Brother Mumpower," replied Mag with a note of bitterness, "ever since't the fust night I've knowed what was the trouble. Ye can set it down, they ain't goin' to be no outpourin' in this meetin'."

"What d'ye think's hinderin', Sister?"

"Why, a preacher orn't to have to ax a ol' woman sich a question! Can't ye see it yerself? I tell ye, so long as they's an on-repentin' an' on-punished murderer a-goin' loose within a mile of the church, they ain't goin' to be no work of grace! They's scripter fer it!"

Gabe Mumpower was troubled. "Mis Tollett," he blurted, "I can't blame ye none fer havin' hard feelin's agin John Cutshaw, but I'm goin' to tell ye somethin' ye ort to know. I'm feelin' called to tell ye."

"Say yer say," answered Mag, closing the Bible and pushing her spectacles back upon her white temples.

"I've been to see John. His mother sent fer me this mornin'."

"Well, I 'lowed he'd be sendin' fer a preacher."

"When I got thar, he was layin' on the bed. I wouldn't 'a' knowed him, he ain't no more than a shadder. His face was as white as the pillercase, 'ceptin' whar the coal dust was ground in under the hide. He was in deep trouble. Said he'd been a turrible wicked man in his time an' ort by rights to 'a' been hung."

"Huh!" sniffed Mag. "Why didn't he tell ye somethin' ye didn't know?"

"Well, I seed he was under powerful conviction. Hit had come on him hard, an' all of a suddent. I axed him why he couldn't turn all holts loose an' make his callin' an' election sure. He kep' a-groanin' an' a-goin' on like a hoss with the colic, an' finally he up an' told me what was holdin' him back."

There was a pause. "Well, go on. I'm hearin' ye." Mag's voice was strangely muffled.

"He said they'd told him what was writ on Tom's monument stone, an' them words kep' a-rising' up betwixt him an' his Maker."

"Ain't them words true, Brother Mumpower?"

"I'm not sayin' they ain't, Sister. I'm only tellin' ye they're risin' up like a cloud in the face of a man that's tryin' to crawl back from the door of hell!"

"Well, they ain't nothin' I can do about it. He killed my boy, an' I gravened it thar on the rock jest like it was. What I have writ I have writ! That's in the Book, too!"

"Mis' Tollett," said Gabe Mumpower rising. "I didn't come to argy with ye. Ye're a good woman an' ye've bore a heap in yer time. Ye kep' back yer boys from violence, an' ye saved John Cutshaw's body from bein' plugged full of holes. I'm axin' ye, will ye do anything to save his soul?"

Courtesy of the Great Smoky Mountains National Park   Photographed by Charles S. Grossman

Little Cataloochee Baptist Church near Coggins Branch. The graveyard has been cleared of grass and the graves have been decorated with tissue paper flowers.

Granny Mag leaned forward in her chair. She gripped the old Bible until the leaders in her knotty hands stood out like rawhide thongs. "No! I won't! That's axin' too much, Preacher! I'm willin' to let him die in his bed, but he'll have to take what's comin' to him hereafter, or do his own dickerin' with the Almighty!"

With flashing eyes she sat and watched the gaunt figure of Gabe Mumpower disappear round the bend of the road.

Tripping down the hillside came Dilsie from the orchard, her apron full of apples. She met her grandmother coming out of the lean-to with a mattock and a spade.

"I'm needin' ye, Dilsie. Fetch that bucket of whitewash an' the brush. We've fooled long enough about fixin' up yer pappy's grave. Let's go an' do it right now."

Under the sultry afternoon sun the mountain girl and the taciturn grandmother dug and shoveled the stony clay about the base of the leaning stone. For some time they worked in silence.

"Granny," timidly ventured the girl finally, "ye're vexed about somethin'. What's happened?"

"Nothin', only the preacher come while ye was up yander. He got me aggervated."

"What about, Granny?"

"A-goin' on with a rigamarole about John Cutshaw bein' like to die an' gittin' oneasy about his soul."

"What did the preacher want ye to do, Granny?"

"He didn't jest say plain out, but he hinted like I ort to scratch this here writin' off'n the rock. I told him p'int blank I wouldn't do no sich!"

The women were through with their task at last. The tombstone stood once more erect, flaunting its damning legend in the faces of the passers-by. The newly whitewashed palings gleamed starkly against the greensward.

"Ye'd better quit an' set a spell, Granny," urged Dilsie when they had returned to the house. "Ye ain't feelin' well enough to keep prodjeckin' so in the br'llin' sun."

"Shet up Dilsie! Quit pesterin' me! I ain't ailin'!" snapped Mag. She would not sit down but roamed through the three rooms of the cabin restlessly. She took a lapful of beans to the porch and began to string the pods for drying, but presently rose from her chair as if startled, scattering the beans everywhere. Finally she went again to the lean-to, seized a hoe, and started climbing the steep path that led from the kitchen dooryard to the corn patch above the orchard.

"Granny, ye'll git a sunstroke!" cried Dilsie in futile protest. "Let me go and chop them weeds fer ye!"

"Let me alone, I tell ye!" snarled Mag. "I'm needin' to stir. My liver's out of fix."

For two hours, until the long shadows of the hemlocks began to fall aslant the corn rows, she plied the hoe "like killin' snakes." Dilsie, down in the kitchen, could hear the sharp chink of the heavy tool on the flinty gravel.

At sunset, exhausted in body and perturbed in spirit, Mag limped down to the cabin. Leaving supper untasted, she changed to her dingy black percale "go-to-meeting" dress, and began the nightly burnishing of the lantern globe. Dilsie, in discreet and anxious silence, donned her own pink lawn frock and awaited orders. They came promptly: "Come on, Honey. Let's hit the trail fer preachin'."

Gabe Mumpower was in perfect form that night. The sermon was but a variation upon the never-failing theme, his stock in trade, the terrors of the judgment. "Whar ye goin' to be Sinner?" He cast the challenge in the faces of the immobile men before him. "Whar ye aimin' to hide yerself that day when the mountains is a-burnin', the sea a-bilin', the sun a-darknin', the moon a-bleedin', an' the stars a-fallin'?"

A score of rough-clad men, who had on previous nights been beguiled into some minor expression of concern, were tonight in their accustomed places, dully waiting to see if anything was going to come of it.

The four Tolletts had attended with unwonted regularity, although they had as yet fallen into none of the snares set for their feet. Only once had there flashed a momentary change of expression across their faces. That was when Mag had risen one night and piped in a tinny treble, "I'm axin' the prayer of all fer four that's outside the Ark of Safety!" The sons had exchanged embarrassed, half-resentful glances, but not a muscle had twitched.

The preacher was in the "weavin' way." "Ol' Satan's the meanest, lowdownest, sorriest, orneriest critter they is anywhars! Ever'n he sees pore sinners wrastlin' under conviction, why here he comes a-rippin' an' a-tearin', a-pitchin' an' a-rarin', to keep 'em from gittin' away!"

"He's shore givin' the devil down-the-country to-night!" whispered Red Jim soberly to Zeb, who nodded in grave approval.

"Folkses," the swarthy giant went on, "I sot today by the beside of a murderer. He tuck the life of a man that hadn't done him no wrong. Fer five year he's been in a endurin' tarmint. He's been shet up in a black pit 'way down under a mountain, diggin' in the dark like a mole; then the cold hand of livin' death laid holt on him, an' hit's been chokin' the good breath out'n him till today he can't raise his head off o' the piller. Afore tomorrer night he's lookin' to go down into a more darker pit than a coal mine, and they ain't nary streak of light, 'ceptin' the awful blue blazes of damnation a-lickin' an' a-creepin' hither an' yan an' leavin' it darker than ever. That's what the deathbed of a murderer is like, an' hit plumb tuck the heart out of me to set thar!"

The listeners had grown tense. The shuffling of boots on the floor ceased. A creaking bench became still.

"But, People, listen! They's worse things than killin' a man's body, even the fine, strengthy body of a young man! They's sech a thing as standin' in the way of a dyin' man a-makin' his peace with the Great Jedge. That's murderin' a man's soul! I'm puttin' it to ye mighty plain, hit's murderin' a man's soul an' sendin' it straight to hell!"

There was a sudden stir. The clack of hard heels on the floor caused a general craning of necks. Mag Tollett was clumping toward the door. Her head was up, her shrunken jaws set tight.

Gabe Mumpower paused, abashed. "Sister Tollett," he called, "ye'll be needed to wrestle in prayer when the mourners come forward. I'd be proud if ye could stay."

Mag neither slowed her pace nor turned her head as she threw back her answer. "I'm goin' home! I've got obleeged to!"

The four sons looked on curiously, but kept their seats as she passed out at the door and banged it after her. They heard the scratch of a match as she lighted the lantern outside. Gabe Mumpower was taken aback. He had intended only to point a moral, but Granny Mag, he now felt, had taken his allusion to John Cutshaw as an accusation and an insult. In a moment, however, he had recovered his composure and renewed his barrage against the devil and his works.

With words that cut and stung and blistered, he lashed the unbelieving. With whips of scorn he harried them. Dull eyes widened with new-born terror. In the circling, flail-like arms whirled the flaming swords of omnipotent wrath. Presently Zeb Tollett's shaggy black head was lowered upon his big hands crossed on the back of the bench ahead. It was Zeb's first sign of weakening.

Up the rough trail to the cabin Mag Tollett strode resolutely. She took off her bonnet to catch in her face the night breeze coming down from the gap. Not once on the stiff climb did she halt for breath.

Reaching the gate, she passed round the house and unlatched the door of the lean-to. In a moment she came out carrying a great sledge hammer that Dave Tollett had used at his forge. Crossing the road and the creek, she clambered over the pasture fence and trudged over to the grassy knoll. The lantern cast ghostly shadows as the grim-visaged woman stepped into the whitewashed enclosure. Ghoul-like she planted her feet at the head of the grave and began hammering the face of the chiseled slab. Her slight frame staggered under the weight of the sledge. Her breath came in panting "ah's" that were partly sobs.

A jagged sliver flew off the edge of the slab. A dozen more clanging blows, and the whole stone was criss-crossed with cracks. Suddenly it fell to pieces, splintered into a thousand shapeless chips. The panting sobs rose into a piteous cry. "O Tommy, Boy, ye understand, don't ye? I'm goin' to put ye a purty boughten stone o' remembrance here, like yer baby's been a-beggin' me to!"

Seizing the lantern she almost ran out of the enclosure. As she passed the gate, she hurled the hammer into the yard and set out again down the trail to the meeting-house.

The sermon was over. In front of the pulpit a group of "mourners" knelt while the "singin' chor" doled out the refrain, "Where will ye spend eternity?" Gabe Mumpower had come down from the pulpit and was going from one to another of the group, his fervent exhortations sounding above the choir's refrain.

Conspicuous among the kneeling figures was the ungainly bulk of Zeb Tollett, with Red Jim beside him. The preacher laid his ponderous hand upon their heads. "Lord bless ye, Brethren," he said kindly. "I wis't yer ol' mother was here to see you-uns a-grievin' fer yer sins. Hit would set her shoutin' fer joy!"

The door opened and Mag Tollett entered. She tiptoed forward and eased softly into her seat beside Dilsie. Gabe Mumpower scanned her features anxiously. Quickly, he was reassured. With the keen penetration of a mountain prophet, he saw that she was wholly changed. Her lips were no longer drawn. A great peace sat upon her time-scarred face.

"People," the preacher's roar had sunk to a low rumble, "you-uns all know they's been somethin' holdin' back this meeting' all the way 'long. Well, jest about twenty minutes ago they was somethin' happened. I don't know exactly what it was, but I naterly felt somethin' bust! They's goin' to be singin' an shoutin' on Thunderin' Creek afore this night's over! Sister Tollett, I sorty think ye've got somethin' laid on yer heart to say to this people. I want ye should git up an' say it!"

Brokenly Mag Tollett rose. She seemed very old, very tired, but her voice shrilled to the farthest corner of the room. "Folks' I reckon I can tell ye what it was that busted awhile ago. I busted it! Yes, I tuck a hammer an' busted it all to shiveration! An' Preacher, they ain't no rock ner no writin' ner nothin' standin' in the way of nobody a-comin' through now. Nobody a-tall, d'ye understand?"

FOR THE HIGH DOLLAR

The drivers of the two cars sat and glowered at each other after the crash. Most of the glowering was done by the big man in the sedan with the Pennsylvania license plates. He was a beefy, bull-necked, bulbous-nosed specimen of Porcus Viensis—which is the botanical name for road hog.

The girl at the wheel of the other car—a smart roadster whose metal tags bore the proud name Virginia, spelled out in full—had turned first to make sure that the gray-haired, soldierly-looking man in the seat beside her was unhurt. Assured of this she calmly waited for the other driver to say something.

Obviously there wasn't much he could say. He simply hadn't given half the road, to which fact the position as well as the state of the two machines bore silent but eloquent testimony. As for the girl—well, she just wasn't taking the ditch today, thank you. The Dixie Highway is wide enough for any two cars to pass, and Ann Houston wouldn't meekly run into the gutter for any road hog. And her aged companion, who might have been—and was—an ex-Confederate captain, felt the same way about it.

After some minutes of blustering and bluffing Porcus Viensis finally mumbled an admission that he carried liability insurance, and produced a card bearing his name and address: "J. Brindel, 408-412 Argyle Street, Philadelphia. Dealer in Antiques."

Meanwhile a sizable crowd had gathered. The crash had occurred in the outskirts of the sequestered village of Boonesboro, Tennessee, where the bumping together of two flivvers is a news item and a collision of "furrin" cars is an event good for two columns in "The Weekly Beacon."

Willing hands pushed the disabled machines to the nearby garage. The bewhiskered mechanic leisurely surveyed the crumbled fenders, bent axles, and wrenched steering gear, spat thoughtfully, and opined that "both cyars mought be ready for the road in three, four hours, mebbe." And that was how it happened that three strangers were left to find whatever of interest might be unearthed in the straggling hamlet nestling at the foot of Great Smoky.

Not that it was a dull day in Boonesboro, however. Nay verily. It was the high tide of activity and excitement. Court was in session. From the river bottoms to the shut-in coves the whole countryside, lawyers and litigants, jurors and witnesses, horse-traders and produce-buyers, everybody who had any business and twice as many who had none, had come to town. The streets were lined with rusty cars, wobbly buggies, and covered wagons. The bray of the mule blended with the honk of the flivver in the general clamor.

In the midst of the tide of noise, confusion, and dust, like an island of shade and comparative calm, rose the quaint old courthouse. Its dinky cupola above the columns of patched plaster towered almost as high as the great maples that surrounded it. The grassy yard was thronged with folk who could not find standing space inside the sweltering courtroom.

The crowd milled about restlessly. Little groups formed here and there, howdying, gossiping, wisecracking. Every little while the shifting throng would be brought to attention by the voice of the sheriff issuing a summons from a second-story window: "Oyez! Oyez! Richard Forgy! Come into Co-o-urt!"

Ann Houston and her grandfather, Captain Stafford, of Abingdon, Virginia, strolled into the courthouse yard, up the stone steps, and into the crowded lobby. The place reeked of stale tobacco juice and the pipe-smoke of yesteryear. Near the foot of the stairway was a bulletin board covered with legal notices—advertisements for bids on road construction, lists of delinquent taxpayers, notices of public sales, and speaking dates of political aspirants.

One notice, scrawled in a bold though unpracticed hand, was attracting considerable attention among the hangers-on. Presently Ann and the Captain edged closer and the girl read the notice aloud. The legal phraseology was stiff and formal enough, but the spelling was delightfully unhampered by convention:

> WHEREAS on the 5th day of Oct. 1928 one Elrod Kimery and his wife Sarmintha Kimery did convey bargain and sell to the undersined Trustee the hereinafter discribed proppery to secure one Jas Arwood the paymint of a certain note for forty-five ($45) dollars, and
>
> WHEREAS said Kimery and wife has defalted in the paymint of said note,
>
> NOW THEREFAR, by vertue of the athorrity vested in me as Trustee, I will expose and offer for sail at high noon in front of the Coarthouse in Boonesboro on the 16 day of June, 1930, at pubic outcry for the high doller the aforementioned proppery, to-wit:
>
> 2 bedstids; 1 stoave and vessels; 2 tables; 1 childs cradle; 1 burow; 5 plane chars; 1 rocken chare; 1 cubbord.
>
> This the 6 day of May, 1930.
>
>   Alex Hansford,
>   Trustee.

"Why, Granddad," exclaimed the girl jokingly, "How exciting! This sale is today, June sixteenth! And it's only a few minutes until high noon! Let's go out and see the proceedings. I've never attended a public sale before."

"I did, once," the Captain replied with a queer little smile. "Only, your grandmother and I weren't just spectators on that occasion. We had to play the role that one Elrod Kimery and his wife Sarmintha will be playing today."

"Oh yes, I've heard mother tell about that. It happened before she was born, didn't it?"

"Yes, some years before. Your grandmother and I were married just before I went to the War. When I got back everything had happened. The slaves were gone, the horses had been stolen, our barns had been burned, and our money was worthless. I tried to hold things together but it couldn't be done. We finally had to sell most of our furniture at auction in order to re-stock the farm. A public sale has never been exactly a sporting event for me since that."

"I know, Granddad. Mother used to tell me of the lovely old things she should have inherited but didn't. Some of them had come from England, hadn't they? And most of them had been in the family since before the Revolution. I wonder if the Kimery's, whoever they are, are giving up their heirlooms. The list on the bulletin board doesn't seem pretentious, but it would mean a lot if it were everything one had."

Outside two men were arranging sundry articles of furniture along the iron fence inside the yard.

"There's the stuff to be sold, evidently," remarked the Captain as he and Ann followed the crowd toward the spot.

The "household goods" proved to be a pathetic assortment of the poorest of poor-white domestic equipment. The bedsteads were rickety affairs with wooden slats. The "chares" were third-rate specimens of the native chairmaker's art, with sagging splint-bottoms. The kitchen cupboard, of quaint three-cornered design, was black with years of wood smoke and encrustations of fly-specks. The ancient relic gave off a heavy mixed odor of parched coffee, garlic, and rancid bacon.

The largest piece of all was the one listed as a "burow." It seemed strangely out of place in the lowly company it was keeping. To be sure, it was as sadly weathered and scarred as any of its fellows, yet any novice must instantly have recognized it as a product of the true cabinet-maker's skill.

It really wasn't a bureau at all, but an old-fashioned chest of drawers. Ann quickly placed the piece as "American Empire," a style somewhat uncommon in the South but occasionally found among the descendants of the pioneers.

It was of beautiful black walnut. The carcase was massive, with paneled ends, and rested upon heavy bracket feet. Its only ornamentation was a chaste oval carved in each panel and a delicate astragal beadwork from top to bottom of the otherwise plain corner posts. The brass pulls were black with tarnish. The whole piece was dingy and discolored as if it might have sat for years in a room where cooking, eating, washing, and all other domestic activities went on.

"Oh, Granddad!" Ann whispered. "Look at that Empire chest! It's a pitiful old wreck, but isn't it a dream!"

"The last link, probably, that binds their present poverty to a forgotten prosperity," the Captain mused aloud.

"Here comes the Kimery family," Ann went on. "Their poor home has been stripped to the walls and floors. Everything they've inherited or acquired to make life a bit easier, piled up and sold to satisfy a wretched little debt, most likely to some skinflint landlord for the rent of a worn-out hillside field."

"I think I know the feeling," the gray-haired warrior answered softly.

There was a stir in the crowd, and a florid giant in a flashy striped suit shouldered his way through the gate and mounted an upturned box. It was easy to guess that he was the redoubtable Alex. Hansford, Trustee. His voice was like a bull of Bashan.

"Ladies an' gents," he boomed. "Pursant to notice published accordin' to law, hit becomes my painful duty to expose an' offer for sale the property here displayed, to satisfy a debt of one Elrod Kimery an' wife to one James Arwood. The terms of the sale is strickly cash in hand, an' ever'thing goes fer the high dollar!"

The spectators crowded around the improvised auction block. Loafers from the street swelled the throng. Court had adjourned for the day and the yard was filled with on-lookers.

"Step right this way, ladies an' gents," called the auctioneer. "Here's yer chanst to pervide yer home with some good, plain, substanshual furnichoor fer purt' nigh nothing'. As the feller says, 'Some goes up an' some goes down, but hit all goes in a lifetime'."

Ann Houston was watching the family of Elrod Kimery. The husband and father sat on a bench and bit off a big chew of tobacco. Sarmintha vigorously plied her snuff-stick. The children, too numerous to count, were scattered around promiscuously, ranging from a grown boy or so to a round-eyed nursling that sprawled on the grass at his mother's feet.

The leather-lunged auctioneer now focused attention upon one of the bedsteads. "Here we are, ladies an' gents! D'ye see this nice, well-made bedstid? Nothin' fancy ner fine, but stout an' stiddy as a new one, an' goin' fer whatever you say! I 'low they's some young folks in this crowd that's aimin' to git spliced a-Sunday. Here's yer chanst to make a start on furnishin' yer new home. Step right up an' look it over!"

A hubbub of titters greeted this pleasantry. A gawky stripling who had been covetously eyeing the furniture from afar now edged closer. Another titter ran through the crowd. Everybody knew that Daly Macklin had been "talking to" Arleeny McDannell for some months and that a wedding was in the offing.

"How much am I offered fer this bedstid?" roared the auctioneer. "Talk up, folks—this is my busy day!"

"Two dollar an' a half!" the youth ventured timidly.

"Aw shucks, now, Daly!" Hansford protested in mock indignation. "What ye want to waste my time fer? Make me a real offer, some of you fellers that wants a bedstid!"

"Three dollar!" a middle-aged farmer, a "widder-man," spoke up, at which the tittering began all over again.

"Three an' a half!" Daly came back, a bit louder this time.

"Four dollar!" the "widder-man" countered after a pause.

"Sakes alive, folks!" the auctioneer called out satirically. "Here's a couple of fellers that wants me to jes' give 'em a fine bedstid fer a weddin' present!"

"Four an' a half!" Daly piped boldly. His competitor hung back and after a moment walked away. The bedstead was "knocked down" to Daly Macklin, who carried it aside.

The second bedstead, the chairs, and the rust stove were quickly disposed of. The cupboard went to the "widder-man" for fifty cents. The child's cradle was next brought forward. It was a rough box, about four feet by two, and a foot and a half in depth, mounted on home-made rockers. Again Hansford waxed facetious.

"Now we're gettin' down to cases, folks! Where's Daly Macklin gone to? Oh, there he is under that tree, guardin' his new bedstid! Come back here, Daly! Here's the rest of yer bedroom 'sweet'!"

Daly came forward, greeted with guffaws by the male portion of the crowd. In a moment he was declared the successful bidder against the "widder-man" for the cradle. He calmly bore it away and placed it beside the bedstead. Sarmintha's dull eyes followed the cradle until it disappeared from view. When she turned her face to the auctioneer again he had placed the chest of drawers beside the block.

Ann Houston noted instantly that the mountain woman's expressionless face had visibly softened. The parting look at the old heirloom, which despite years of incredible abuse and neglect, had grown to be a piece of the poor creature's heart—this, the girl divined, had been too much for even a cave woman's Spartan calm. Ann's own heartstrings were taut with the tug of the mute tragedy.

Sarmintha turned an appealing gaze upon the auctioneer, and her close-set lips worked convulsively for a second. Then with a sob she buried her face in her knotty hands. A twinge of pity must have stirred the heart of Alex. Hansford, Trustee. At any rate his manner changed. His cheap badinage was gone entirely as he proceeded to dispose of the last remaining article.

"Now, ladies an' gents, they's jest one thing left. I've been keepin' it back fer the last an' best. Hit's this nice, handsome burer, which ever' one of you will agree is a plumb elegant piece of furnichoor fer any home in the county."

The crowd showed signs of deepening interest. Several women, wives of comfortable farmers, began to inspect the chest critically. Meanwhile Hansford's attention was drawn to a beefy, bull-necked, bulbous-nosed stranger who had pushed his way forward. Ann touched her grandfather's arm.

"See, Granddad," she whispered, "there's our friend the road hog. He has a wicked gleam in his eye. I miss my guess if he isn't watching this chance to gobble up this relic."

"Well, he'll be able to grab it off for next to nothing," the Captain replied. "There won't be much competition."

Ann felt a flush of indignation. "It's none of my business, of course, but it fairly makes me boil to see him drop in here and pick up a genuine antique for nothing, just because none of these people have the slightest idea of its value."

"Well, here we go, folks!" Hansford was shouting. "What am I offered fer the burer? Made of genuwine walnut, the solidest, lastiest wood they is! Most likely a hunderd year old, an' good fer another hunderd! How much am I bid?"

"Five dollars!" a decent-looking farmer announced after his wife had whispered something in his ear.

"I'll make it seven!" another called promptly.

"Eight!"

"Eight-fifty!"

The first bidder bent to hear another word from his wife, then shook his head. Hansford waited a moment, mopped his brow, and began his professional intonation. "Eight an' a half, ladies an' gents, fer a beautiful burer ye couldn't buy new fer forty over there at the Beehive Store! Why, folks, are ye goin' to let this unheard-of bargain go fer a mere handful of chicken-feed. Come on, now, good people, an' look at it!"

The canny hill folk looked, but nobody raised the bid. Hansford kept up a sonorous harangue after the manner of his kind, but the bidding was over.

"Eight-fifty! Do I hear nine? Somebody give me nine! Well, then, eight-fifty! Eight-fifty once't! Eight-fifty twice't! Eight—"

"Nine dollars!" a new voice interposed. The voice had a brisk foreign quality that contrasted sharply with the flat drawl of the natives. The mountaineers started, craning their necks to see the stranger. For the second time that day Ann Houston frowned into the face of J. Brindel, of Philadelphia, Dealer in Antiques.

"Now that's more like it, folks!" Hansford exclaimed.

"Nine dollars I'm offered by a gentleman that knows a good piece of furnichoor when he sees it! Now who'll make it ten?"

Nobody spoke, though people jostled one another for a better look. Hansford harangued a little more and finally began: "Nine dollars once't! Nine dollars twice't! Nine—"

Then a woman's voice spoke, quietly but clearly.

"Twenty dollars!"

The words thrilled through the crowd like an electric shock. Even the hardboiled auctioneer gasped, but only for the fraction of a second.

"That's business now, ladies and gent! They's some folks here that knows furnichoor. The lady bids twenty dollars. What do you say, good people?"

"Fifty!" J. Brindel's face was red with annoyance and determination as he spat the words out viciously.

"One hundred!" Ann Houston called as quietly as before.

Elrod Kimery had stopped chewing. He stood transfixed, the tobacco quid bulging one cheek like a tumor. Sarmintha lifted her eyes, red with weeping, and stared in amazement.

"Hundred and fifty!" Brindel shot back angrily. "And that's twice what the blamed reproduction's worth!"

"Two hundred!" came Ann's even-voiced response.

The onlookers were dumfounded. A group of unshaven swains took it as a huge joke and burst into hoarse laughter. Brindel, his face like a thundercloud, shrugged his shoulders and sidled away as if leaving the scene.

"Two hundred dollars!" Hansford chanted. "Two hundred once't! Twice't! Three—"

The disgruntled dealer in antiques, however, wasn't yet ready to give up a genuine American Empire. He turned on his heel and snapped a final offer: "Two twenty-five!" And he almost shook his fist in Ann's face.

But Ann was done. Truth to tell, she hadn't really set out to bid the piece in, notwithstanding she had a patrician's taste for such things and the money to gratify it withal. Uppermost had been her grim resolve to foil the little game of Porcus Viensis and make him pay a fair price for what she knew he so greedily coveted. She felt a flow of elation—she had made him pay!

"Two twenty-five!" roared the auctioneer. "Two twenty-five once't! Twice't! Three times! Going—"

"Two hundred and fifty!" a new voice broke in. It was a man's voice.

Hansford whistled in undisguised amazement this time. J. Brindel looked like something that had been hit with a brick. Ann couldn't believe her ears. Was that really Granddad's voice? Then she saw he had slipped away and was standing beside the chest of drawers. His hands were toying with one of the blackened brass pulls. She hadn't been mistaken.

Hansford's closing formula was droning in her ears: "Two fifty once't! Twice't! Three times! Going, going, and gone! Gone, ladies an' gents to the old gentleman here! The sale is now closed!"

The country folk began to disperse but their tongues wagged merrily.

"By grab, Nathe, did ye ever see the beat?"

"Never in life! What in thunder do them crazy nuts want with that ol' thingamajig anyhow?"

"Aw, them city folks goes plumb looney over old things jes' because they air old. Why, a feller from Knoxville give me ten dollars once't fer an ol' rusty candle-mould, an' us been usin' coal-ile lamps for thirty year!"

"Well, anyhow, this shore was a lucky day fer Elrod an' Sarminthy!"

When Ann reached her grandfather's side he was counting off a roll of bills into the receptive palm of Alex. Hansford, Trustee, who in turn was scrawling the grand old word "Paid" across the face of Kimery's note to James Arwood. He then delivered to Elrod the balance of two hundred-odd dollars in cash. Elrod had resumed his chewing and he stuck the roll into his pocket as nonchalantly as if such transactions were of daily occurrence. Sarmintha's face was a study in gray.

Ann could hold in no longer. "Why, Granddad, what on earth? Didn't you see my game? I knew the Great Hog was simply bound to have that chest, and I made up my mind he was going to pay for it!"

Courtesy of the Great Smoky Mountains National Park

Baby's cradle - 1936. Notice the woman's shoes in the left background behind the quilt.

"Oh, yes, I saw that," the old soldier smiled. "But all at once I got interested in the case and decided to take a little hand myself."

The crowd had gone now except Elrod, Sarmintha, and the youngest Kimery, who clung tight to his mother. The look of dazed wonder in the mountain mother's lusterless eyes broke through the Virginia girl's reserve. Impulsively she threw her arm about Sarmintha's shoulder.

"My dear, it was cruel to hurt you so! But we were only trying to see that you got what it was worth."

Sarmintha gave her a puzzled look. Then a light of understanding broke, and with a smile.

"Law, Missy, ye mean that ol' clo'es press? Why bless yer soul, honey, I wouldn' 'a' hauled hit home fer it!"

"But, my dear, you cried when they put it up to be sold."

"No, no, Missy! That weren't what I was blubberin' about! But when they rifled off my ol' cradle I jes' had to cry a little, ridic'lous as it was. I've rocked 'leven younguns in that cradle. Hit don't look like I'll never have no more, fer the last un's two year old past. I got to thinkin' about never havin' no more babies to nuss ner no cradle to rock, an' hit jes' sorty upsot me!"

"But doesn't it hurt you to give up this fine old chest of drawers that must have been in the family for generations?"

"Law no, Missy! I'm proud to get shet of it. I like purty things myself, not ol' wore-out things like that. D'ye see that fine purty burer in the Beehive store over yander?" She pointed to an ornate factory-made dresser in a show-window across the street. "Ever' time I come to town I crave hit like I crave a seat in Heaven! We're goin' to buy it today, an' a brass bed with bouncy springs on it, an' a set of fotchon cheers—ain't we, Elrod?"

The master of the house nodded approval. "Yeah, this here money jes' sorty drapped down from some'rs, as ye might say, an' if she wants to buy the whole durn store full of fixin's, she can have em!"

"Well, I'm so glad for you!" Ann said with a mist of joyous tears in her eyes. "But by the way, could you tell us the history of the old chest? It must have a real story connected with it."

"No, ma'am, hit hain't got much hist'ry. They was a young captain up in Virginny—I disremember his name—that was broke up right atter the Civil War an' had to sell his furnishments. My paw was a tenant on the place an' he bid in this ol' press at the sale. Then he moved to Tennessee an' fotch it along, an' we couldn't git rid of it."

Ann began to see the light. "Why, Granddad, you mean you recognized—"

"Come, dear, we must be going," he answered a bit brusquely to conceal the tremor in his voice. But as they moved away he confided softly: "Of course I recognized it! I should have known it in China!"

At the garage they found their car ready. "The big feller got his'n 'bout half a hour ago," the mechanic chuckled. "He 'peared plumb peeved about somethin'. 'Lowed he didn't never want to see ner hear tell of this durn little jumpin'-off place no more!"

"Too bad!" Ann declared. "Something must have spoiled the day for him! But he helped to make it a happy day for us!"

WHAT IS TO BE WILL BE

The first thing Penelope Wilson had to do when she came to be the mistress of the little mountain school in Chinquapin Cove was to get used to being called "Miss Pennylope." The next and much harder job she tackled was to learn the names, faces, and degrees of consanguinity of the legion of young Tadlocks who thronged the tiny schoolhouse. As Old Doc Wheeler, the unlettered Aesculapius of Chinquapin, declared, "the sassafras, wild ingerns, an' Tadlocks had plumb *took* Bumpass county."

Penelope soon discovered, however, that most of the rising generation whose names she registered were the lineal descendants of Squire Hamp Tadlock, whose two-story log house was the geographical, political, and theological hub of the Chinquapin settlement.

"Uncle Hamp" and his aged helpmeet, Geraldine, lived their sunset years in unbroken calm. Hard toil of their youth and prime had brought them comfort as comfort is reckoned in the Tennessee coves. Their sons and daughters with their families lived about them in the valley and did the old man's bidding. One son only, Dave, the youngest and most restless, had moved to North Carolina and settled on Cataloochee, in the shadow of Great Smoky.

The rest had remained to replenish the earth in the ancestral cove. Consequently Penelope had enrolled five lusty Hamp Tadlocks, whom she learned to distinguish as Big Hamp, Little Hamp, Bill's Hamp, Luther's Hamp, and Wormy Hamp. After that all went well.

There was one little Tadlock, however, whom Penelope discovered one day, though his name wasn't on her school roll, nor, so she was assured, could ever be on any school roll. For D. Boone Tadlock, aged eight, youngest and widest-eyed of Jake's flock, knew the big world only as it peeped at him from the outside as he lay upon his pallet on the cabin floor, or perhaps on the sunny front porch on pretty days.

Old Doc Wheeler had long ago pronounced his verdict with grave shaking of his head. "His hip j'nts ain't made like they ort to be. They ain't nothin' to do about it, but he can't never walk."

D. Boone knew that his poor, twisted legs could never carry him through the gate and up the wooded ridge of Cattail Knob that walled in his narrow world. His deep brown eyes, though, missed little that went or came in the wonder-world that was ever thronging over Jake's paling fence and through the windows and doors or the cracks in the chinking of the log walls.

Penelope had loomed upon the lad's horizon soon after her arrival. She was the first "furriner" he had ever known. She came from a great city of fully five thousand people inconceivably far away—a hundred miles, they said. And she was a gradjiate of the State College! But for all she was so citified and so eddicated, folks soon found out she was "jist as common as a rail fence," which is as fine a compliment as we can ever pay you in Chinquapin Cove.

A day or so after Penelope's first visit to the crippled child she made it convenient to pass Jake Tadlock's house just when she knew she would find Jake and Phrony, his wife, out in the milking lot. While Phrony milked, Penelope sat on a barrel and talked about little D. Boone.

"He's a wonderful child!" she declared. "I've never seen a finer head or more intelligent eyes. You should certainly have him examined by a specialist. They're making remarkable cures of such cases nowadays. I want you to let me write to a splendid doctor I know in Nashville and ask his advice."

A sudden gleam of hope leaped into Phrony's eyes as she looked up from her milking stool. "O Miss Pennylope! D'ye reckon they could make him so's he could walk? The Good Lord knows how proud I'd be!"

There was the faintest glimmer of animation in Jake's voice as he replied. "Much ableeged, Ma'am. Hit's kind of ye to proffer that. Howsomeever, I'd do nothin' without axin' Paw. I'll name it to him the fust time he draps in."

It chanced that Penelope was making one of her frequent calls to see her little protege when the Squire "drapped in." Jake came bluntly to the point. "Paw, Miss Pennylope 'lows D. Boone mought git fixed up if we sent him to one of them big doctors out yander. Me an' Phrony's been talkin' it over an' we're might' nigh in the notion, but I aimed to ax you afore we done anythin'."

"No!" The Squire spoke the one word quietly but firmly.

Penelope turned in amazement. "Why, Squire Tadlock! I was just sure you'd be so pleased. Everybody says D. Boone is your favorite grandchild. You'll let him have this chance, won't you?"

"No'm, I'm agin it." The old man's tone was courteous, but there was a ring of finality in it. "Hit ain't nary bit o' use. I've told Jake an' Phrony time an' time agin they won't never raise this one. Hit were the Lord's doin'. What is to be will be. That's Scripture. Some's predestined to have sorror an' trouble, an' we hain't no right to complain."

Deeply hurt, Penelope turned to the parents for backing in a further appeal. Jake's face was a mask. Phrony's eyes were duller and her voice more plaintive than usual as she weakly yielded to the grandfather's patriarchal authority. "Yes, Paw. I reckin ye're right."

"Folks this day an' time," Uncle Hamp went on, "is gettin' so tarnation smart they 'low they can go squar in the face of Godamighty. Jes' like them people in the Good Book that tried to build 'em a tower cle'r up to heaven so's they could set up thar an' laugh at God if He sent another flood."

Penelope would have given up the fight had it not been for the appealing look of the little cripple who was gazing wraith-like upon them as they bandied his fate in their hands.

"Squire Tadlock," she pleaded, "when *you're* sick you send for the doctor. This child is just sick and I'm almost sure the doctors can cure him."

"No, ma'am, this ain't no sickness. This boy was born this way. If hit's the Lord's will fer him to git stout he'll *git* stout. If hit ain't he won't."

The case was settled; that was clear enough. But every day or so the busy schoolmistress of Chinquapin found time to drop in for a chat and a laugh with the little shut-in. Daily she came to comprehend the unconquerable courage of the lad, in whose fragile body beat a heart as stout and resolute as that of the intrepid pioneer whose name he bore. Daily, too, she came to realize how hopeless was her dream of winning for the child his one chance for restoration.

Phrony was a true daughter of the mountains, pliant, cowed, man-tanned, though the feckful daring of the old Indian fighters was in her blood. Jake, too, was at heart a pioneer and an adventurer, but the code of the hill-clans held him fast. "I've allus heeded Paw," he would say. "The old ones knows best. I'll be a grandsire some day an' I expect mine to do as I tell 'em."

Penelope, however, refused to abandon hope. She wrote a forbidden letter to the specialist and a week later had a reply. It offered encouragement, but she kept it to herself. Her own faith in the predestinate schedule of mundane haps and mishaps allowed for a wee bit of diplomacy, by way of helping Providence out in a pinch.

And Penelope was a diplomat. Well she knew that none of the usual wiles of scheming femininity—argument, tears, or flattery—would avail. Hamp Tadlock was woman-proof. Like a good general, then, she decided to storm the Squire's frowning fortress just where he himself believed it to be absolutely impregnable—in the moated and bastioned gate of his rock-ribbed theology.

Through the schoolhouse window Penelope saw the Squire riding past on his claybank mare. Divining his destination she fudged a little on the last spelling lesson and dismissed school early. She found the old man at Jake's house. After a cheery greeting she suddenly asked: "Squire Tadlock, do you know a minister by the name of Tucker?"

"Yes, ma'am. Enoch Tucker. But he's a Methodis'." There was obvious disparagement in the tone.

"Well, he told me today he was going to North Carolina to hold a revival on Cataloochee."

"H'm! Ye don't say! Well, I'm sorry. I've got a boy that lives on Cataloch."

"Yes, I knew that. And Brother Tucker said he was going to look him up and try to get him interested in the meeting."

"That's what werries me, ma'am. Davy ain't well grounded an' rooted in the faith. I mistrust them Methodis'. They're spreadin' the onscriptural doctrines fur an' wide. I'm oneasy they'll git Davy's feet in the miry clay."

"That would surely be a pity," declared Penelope sympathetically. Now the truth is that Penelope was a Methodist herself, but that damning fact had not been noised abroad in Chinquapin Cove. "It certainly looks," she went on soberly, "as though you might have a Methodist in the family."

The old man's eyes flashed with indignation. "No ma'am! I won't that! I've tried to bring up my house in the ways of right, an' I don't aim to see nary one turn out ornery!"

"That's a noble spirit for a father to have," replied Penelope encouragingly, "but I understand the Methodists are strong in Carolina."

"Jes' leave it to me! Jerline an' me will go over thar an' stay till Davy gits his feet planted on the rock, if it takes all winter!"

Jake and Phrony gasped at the sudden decision, but Penelope lent her full moral support. "You're exactly right, Squire! What is to be will be. I believe that myself."

The squire beamed upon her. "I'm proud ye've been fotch up proper, Miss Pennylope. Me an' Jerline is leavin' tomorrer. We'll make it a pertracted visit an' stay till corn-plantin' time."

The grandfather's leave-taking with the crippled grandchild was, for him, unusually demonstrative. "D. Boone, yer grandsire's goin' to be gone a spell. I hope ye'll live an' git stouter, if hit's the Lord's will. An' I'll bring ye a purty when I come back. G'bye, honey!"

Two evenings later Penelope was again at Jake's house. The child had been put to bed in the back room, perchance to dream of racing on flying feet and chasing b'ars and pa'nters.

"I keep thinking about the boy," Penelope led off in that persuasive way she had. "I'm convinced that the only thing in the way of his getting well is our failure to give him his chance."

"O Miss Pennylope!" Phrony burst out passionately. "Ever since ye fust named it I've kep' a-ponderin' it in my mind. Seems like it ain't human to jes' let him go on draggin' hisself through life like a wild critter cotch in a steel trap!"

"No, Phrony," Jake reproved her, "they ain't no use goin' through all that no more. Paw's agin it, an' I dassent contrary him."

Penelope saw that both parents were deeply stirred. Even Jake, dry-eyed and steady-voiced as he was, had an unwonted sadness in his face. There remained but one obstacle, but that was as real and formidable as the granite-ribbed mountain looming above the cabin. There was a moment of silence. The lamplight was a-flicker by the blaze of the logs on the hearth. A creaking of the inner door caused them all to turn. Through the crack of the door the face of the child stared up at them.

"Why, D. Boone, honey, whar ye goin'?" Phrony chided. "We 'lowed ye was asleep a hour ago!"

"No, Maw, I heared Miss Pennylope a-talkin' an' I wanted to hear what she was sayin'."

A sudden inspiration came to Penelope. "Listen! Grandfather Tadlock is right! What is to be will be! And I propose we leave it to D. Boone to settle the question himself. What do *you* want to do, dear, about going to the city doctor? You've heard us talking about it, I know."

Jake had lifted the child in his arms and brought him to the fireside. A light of surprise and understanding broke in the boy's eyes. "Law, Miss Pennylope, hit's funny ye'd ax *me*! 'Course I'd hate to aggrevate Grandpap, but I shore do crave to git my laigs fixed if they's any way it could be! I'd work hard an' pay the money back!"

It was more than Phrony could stand. She wept audibly and unabashed. Jake was fighting in he-man fashion but having a hard time of it. Finally he spoke. "That settles it! If he wants it that bad, I give in, no differ *what* Paw says!"

Courtesy of the Great Smoky Mountains National Park

Smokemont residents witness a baptism in the waters of the Oconaluftee sometime between 1915 and 1920. The preacher and person being baptized are in the lower right.

It was corn-planting time when Uncle Hamp and Geraldine, having seen Davy safely immersed in the waters of Cataloochee, turned their faces back toward Chinquapin. On the homeward journey they stopped in Knoxville, where Uncle Hamp made a mysterious purchase. It was something bulky, and it took two men to lift it in its burlap-lined crate. Two days later Luther Tadlock hauled the crate to his father's house. The Squire refused to gratify idle curiosity. "Jest a whimmididdle to grind smoke with," was all he'd say.

Next day the old couple came to Jake's house, riding in the old farm wagon. The crated thing half filled the wagon bed. Jake came to the gate, greeted the old folks, and helped carry the crate to the porch.

"Whar's D. Boone?" the grandfather asked.

"Why, Miss Pennylope come by in her Ford an' tuck him fer a ride. They'll be back d'rekly."

"That's good, Jake. I promised him a purty when I come, an' I've fotch it. We'll unwrap it afore he gits here. He'll open them big eyes of his'n when he sees it!"

In three minutes Jake and Phrony, with Uncle Hamp and Geraldine, were gazing upon the polished wood, tufted upholstery, and shiny metal fixtures of a thing whose like had never been seen in Chinquapin. It was the latest and most improved wheel chair.

"Why, Paw, what in Creation?" Jake gasped.

"What ye got to say about that?" the Squire demanded, his pride shining in his face.

"Hit's sure the purtiest thing I ever laid my eyes on, Paw!" exclaimed Phrony with the eagerness of a child. "But, Paw, hit's come too late to do D. Boone any good."

The old man's face clouded with distress. "Is that so, Phrony? I'm awful sorry to hear that! I was hopin' he'd git stout enough to roll hisself about in it. But hit's like I've allus told ye. What is to be will be. We mustn't complain."

"We ain't complainin', Paw," answered Phrony half frightened.

A shiny coupe came to a stop at the gate. "Git out thar, Jake, an' tote the little-un in the house," Uncle Hamp ordered.

"Wait a minute, Paw." Jake answered quietly.

The door of the car opened and a small boy in knickers climbed out, a bit stiffly, and came walking with a slight limp up the steps. "Howdy, Grandpap an' Granny!" he shouted, and he waved his hand toward his grandmother.

Geraldine let out a yell and flopped limply into a chair. "Oh Lordy!" she screamed. "For the love o' God, Phrony, am I seein' a ha'nt?"

"Why, Granny, what ails ye?" called the lad as he ran to her. "Hit's me! Ain't ye goin' to say howdy?"

"Git away! Don't tetch me! Hit give me the all-overs!" the old lady shouted hysterically.

"Jerline, ca'm yerself!" Uncle Hamp commanded. "They ain't no sense in a female as old as you a-takin' on that away. What's been goin' on here, Jake? What's you an' Phrony been an' done?"

Jake stammered in embarrassment. He had dreaded this moment for months.

"Why, Paw, hit was Miss Pennylope. She axed *him* what he wanted to do, an' he was so sot on goin' to the doctor that me an' Phrony give in. He was gone three months an' when he come home he could walk a teeny bit. Now he's gittin' stouter ever' week, up an' goin' the whole dawggone day, an' eatin' like a fattenin' hawg!"

"Paw," Phrony broke in, trembling and smiling at the same time, "we shore hated to cross ye, but we tuck a chance fer him. Anyhow, you allus said, 'What is to be will be.' Miss Pennylope said so too!"

Uncle Hamp took a plug of tobacco from his pocket and leisurely bit off a huge chew. "Well, Jake," he said finally, "me an' Miss Pennylope was right, wasn't we? An' I reckon we can trade this here whimmididdle fer a bicycle!"

CORPUS DELICTI

There had never really been any bad blood between Grannison Cole and Sevier Dugger. That is a material fact that might be of prime importance in this tale. Still, there was no love lost between the two burly mountaineers, and that fact, too, has its significance. Doubtless, Grannison felt a sort of proprietorship in Huggins Hell, seeing that his cabin stood at the very edge of that far-flung labyrinth of rhododendron, laurel, and greenbrier. He'd always lived there, and his father before him for that matter.

Grannison knew the Hell better than most of the Smoky folk, too. He knew it well enough to respect, if not to fear, its gloomy immensity, the dark desolation into which the hardiest hillsman ventures only with circumspection and where the tenderfoot has no business—ever.

Huggins Hell has a geography all its own, but its geographers are few. It belongs by right to the raccoon, the bobcat, and the bear. Bear-runs are the only trails that traverse, or ever will traverse, that savage waste. Along these runs, veritable tunnels through the overarching jungle, man and dog do, on occasion, follow bruin by the hour, but the man must go on all fours like the dog and the bear.

Grannison Cole's parting of the ways with Sevier Dugger started with the forking of the bear trail in Huggins Hell. Sevier Dugger, like Grannison, was a veteran hunter. His dogs were among the best in Smoky. But he hunted alone. As any mountaineer will tell you, "they's somethin' quare an' ornery about a feller that hunts by hisself thataway."

Moreover, Sevier Dugger was an outlander, having just trekked into the Sugarlands a few years back "from some furrin place out yander—Catalooch, over in Ca'liny," he said. And yet Sevier seemed to think that Huggins Hell was his personal game preserve. Worse yet, he had recently bragged openly that he was going to bag or kill Old Slewfoot and come home the champion bear hunter of Big Smoky.

Old Slewfoot. There you have it, the sore spot deep hidden inside Grannison Cole's shaggy chest. But probably Sevier Dugger didn't know that. Old Slewfoot, the notorious, elusive black bear of Huggins Hell, had harried the sheep rangers and hog pens of the Sugarlands for near a decade. Incredibly cunning, uncannily invulnerable, he had become a legend of the Smokies, a bit of werewolf lore bruited by the fireside when the night wind came zooming out of the Hell on winter nights.

Once, though, the wily beast had left two toes from his right forepaw in Grannison Cole's steel trap. Since that time his familiar tracks, with the toes missing, had won him his name, Old Slewfoot. And was it any wonder that Grannison felt a certain priority among the mountain Nimrods with respect to the hunting of the rogue?

Moreover, Grannison had lately discovered, while scouting, a new bear-run that branched off out of the deep fissure of the Hell and bore away easterly toward the Sawteeth Gap, leading presumably into the trackless woods on the Carolina side. Grannison believed his discovery solved the mystery of Old Slewfoot's innumerable baffling escapes. He was only waiting the onset of winter to stage a big hunt and prove his theory.

On a late November afternoon Grannison, mending the ga'nt-lot fence, hailed his neighbors, Newt and Zeke Brackins and Jeter Clegg, who chanced along. As the four gassed and gossiped, Sevier Dugger ambled out of the laurel that fringed the jungle and joined the group. He had something on his mind.

"Boys, I've been scoutin' in the Hell all day, an' I found somethin'. I bet I'm the only man in Sugarlands that ever seed it. Hit's a main b'ar-run leadin' 'way off t'wards the Sawteeth. I'm goin' in thar with my dogs at crack o' day tomorrer, an' I'm goin' to have Ol' Slewfoot's hide stretched up on my cow shed afore sundown!"

Zeke Brackins chuckled. "Better men than you has got lost in that tore-down place."

"Yeah, Sevier," admonished Jeter Clegg, "Ol' Slewfoot knows the Hell better than any of us."

Grannison Cole did not join in the banter. His face had darkened with sudden anger. As Sevier turned to go, Cole's only word was a soft-voiced, cryptic warning. "Ye better let that b'ar-run alone. An' remember, I told ye!"

When the Brackins boys and Jeter Clegg had gone, Grannison sat still on the fence. The longer he sat the angrier he grew. "The low-down, ill-born skunk! He's went an' found that new run, an' he'll take him a stand in the Sawteeth Gap an' git my b'ar!" His smoldering anger fused presently into dark and sinister purpose. And purpose, with Grannison Cole, quickly blazed into action.

In a few minutes Mat, his taciturn helpmeet, observed him setting forth with a heavy object slung across his shoulder with a stout chain. "Eh law, thar he goes with that ol' b'ar-trap, an' hit supper time," she grumbled. "Twon't be nothin' but trappin' an' huntin' from now till dawgwood blooms!"

Twilight fell long before Grannison had burrowed his way to the foot of the cliff where the secret runway branched off. For that matter, it is forever twilight in Huggins Hell. But the hunter's eyes, keen as a bobcat's, soon descried a white "blaze" scratched upon a sapling with a knife blade.

It was enough. Dugger had found the runway. Grannison angrily shouldered his way a few yards farther into the brushy tunnel. Clawing with his hands in the black mold, he hollowed out a foot-deep pit. Into this, squarely in the middle of the bear-path, he set the trap. With a stout stick he pried open the notched jaws until they formed a yawning ring of steel at the level of the ground. Cautiously he set the trigger plate in place. The chain he looped around a rhododendron root. A team of horses could not have torn it loose.

Then he sprinkled a light covering of rotted leaves over the deadly circle. No man, scarcely any beast, could have detected the slight disturbing of nature's primordial floor. A cold-blooded thing to do, planting a bear-trap in a trail. A thing abhorred, forbidden by law. Men have languished in prison for it, have swung by the neck for murder thus committed. The best any wretch could hope for, caught so, would be to linger for hours, or days, burning with fever from shattered bone and lacerated flesh until some chance passer-by should come to the rescue.

In Huggins Hell there are no passers-by.

Grannison groped his way homeward by feel. Mat was asleep when he reached the cabin. He fell into bed grimly, exulting in the certain success of his ruse. Sleep, however did not come. Never in his forty years had he spent so wakeful a night on his rough bed.

"Whatever ails ye, Grannison?" Mat inquired fretfully, disturbed by his tossing. "Air they bitin' as bad as all that?"

"Nothin's the matter," he growled. "Shet up, an' let a man git some sleep."

But the hours dragged by, and the eyes of Grannison Cole stared wide in the darkness. Something in his head pounded like the strokes of a clock. His mouth was dry, his nerves were taut and jumpy.

The crowing of the weatherbeaten rooster outside broke the weird stillness preceding dawn. From down the valley came the faint baying of hounds. Grannison's own dogs under the floor answered with long howls, but subsided, snarling, when he hurled maledictions at them from his bed. He lay and listened. Soon a man and a yelping pack passed the house. He heard the clack of hobnailed boots upon the crossing-rocks in the creek bed, heard the clatter muffled into soft crunching footfalls as the man entered the laurel. Thereafter was silence.

Grannison arose, unrested, thirsty, dizzy. He took a stiff drink from a jug in the lean-to and went out-doors. The first gray bars of light were sifting through the fir-tops, but midnight still mantled the great deeps of the Hell. He went to the stable, and fed the "critters"—the raw-boned mule, the brindled cow-brute. The morning breeze blew fresh upon his forehead. His head grew cooler, his temples eased their pounding. And with that, his fury went out of him. Reason returned, and the tremor of a sickening fear.

As the first sunrays flooded the barnyard with half-light, his haggard eyes played tricks with him. The rude stable of poles loomed out of the mist like the walls of the jailhouse. The wooden slats across the haymow were the iron bars of the death cell. The rope-end dangling from the ridge-pole—*ugh!* he well enough knew what that was, too. All the backwoodsman's terror of the law, the prison, the gallows, leaped upon him as a pant'er leaps upon a bleating yearling.

"God A'mighty! What have I went an' done? I can't let a man go on an' die like that. Hit's murder!"

Sweat stood in drops on his face as he realized what he had done—what could not now be undone. Dugger had been on his way an hour, must by now have reached the trap. He could not miss it. Grannison got himself together. In the growing light he straightened up, alert, ready, the man of action, the rough hillsman, hotheaded and vengeful in an hour of sudden rage, yet who could not harbor a cold hate nor plot a crime with malice aforethought. His first impulse was to start instantly to Dugger's rescue, but Mat was now calling him to breakfast.

"Maybe he won't git so bad hurt with them thick cowhide boots of his'n. Anyhow I'll go atter I eat a snack an' I'll fetch him out o' thar."

Breakfast over, he took down his rifle and started out. At the gate he hesitated.

"I'd better take somebody with me. I'll need help to git him down here. Guess I'll step down the holler and ax' the Brackins boys to go with me on a little ja'nt."

Newt and Zeke were cutting pole timber down the valley. Looking up they saw Cole approaching.

"H'lo, Grannison! Ye're jist in time to give us a boost with this ches'nut."

"Shore, Newt," answered Grannison obligingly. "I'll he'p you-uns th'ow this tree an' then I wan't both of ye to he'p me. I've got a little business up in the Hell."

"Right enough. We'll be glad to git to lay off o' this job a spell."

The stately chestnut was toppling, and Grannison thrust a pike pole into the wood to guide its fall. With a ripping sound of tough splinters the bole plunged earthward exactly where the choppers had aimed it. Its lower portion, however, fell across the trunk of an uprooted hemlock, which severed as a fulcrum, tearing the butt loose from its stump. It catapulted backward like a battering-ram, and struck Grannison a glancing blow upon the head, knocking him senseless to the ground.

The brothers dropped axe and saw, and picking up the unconscious man carried him up the bank and laid him on the ground. Finding that the breath was still in him but failing in their efforts to arouse him to speech, the stalwart neighbors bore their stricken comrade down to the wagon road and thence in a straw-filled wagon-bed to the hospital in the settlement at Gatlinburg.

A white-capped nurse was moving about the bed of the big woodsman who for a fortnight had lain in a deathlike torpor. On a sudden the girl noticed a change in the patient's breathing. There was a sort of gasp, a long-drawn sigh, as of one waking from peaceful sleep. The man's eyes opened and looked at her.

"Howdy ma'am," he said weakly. "Whar'd you come from?"

"Why, I've been here all the while," she replied smiling. "But you've had a long, long sleep."

"I reckon I did doze off a little. An' I was dreamin' somethin' turrible!"

Then as the man's mind slowly cleared, he began to take in his strange surroundings. "Say, missy, whar'm I at? This ain't my house!"

"No, you're in the hospital at Gatlinburg. You were hurt by a falling tree two weeks ago and you've just now waked up."

Hospital? Gatlinburg? Falling tree? He couldn't make sense of it. Where was any falling tree! Had he just dreamed it? No, there *had* been a falling tree! And he had pushed with a pike pole, and the tree came down—crash! He couldn't think of the rest of it just now.

"Missy, what day is it?"

"This is Saturday."

"When was it I got hurt?"

"Two weeks ago today."

Through the fog in his brain came a gleam of terrifying recollection. The tall chestnut tumbling to the ground—Zeke and Newt standing there—and, far away, a man hung in a steel trap in a dark tunnel!

"Oh, my God!" the woodsman groaned. "Hit ain't so! Tell me I jes' dreamp it missy!"

The nurse was preparing to administer a quieting hypodermic, but the man shoved her away.

"Git me my clo'es!" he shouted. "I've got business to 'tend to. I'm leavin' here!"

Then he fell back upon the pillow exhausted. Two days later, however, in defiance of doctors and nurses, he strode unsteadily out and caught a teamster's wagon bound for the Sugarlands.

Mat welcomed him with Spartan calm. The Brackinses dropped in to say howdy. Uncle Nelse Walker and Jeter Clegg brought him a squirrel.

"Squirrel broth is strenthenin'," Jeter allowed.

Grannison chuckled, tried to joke, hiding the gnawing anxiety within.

"Any news in these diggin's?" he asked casually. He was afraid to ask, more afraid not to do so.

"B'lieve no," answered Newt. "Ever'thin's about as common. Looks like Sevier Dugger's gone an' left us."

Grannison's heart sank into his boots.

"So? Whar did he say he was goin'?"

"Didn't say. Jest up an' lit out."

"That's quare. Not so quare neither. Ye know he was allus takin' sudden notions."

"Yeah," Brackins went on. "Ye mind he said he was aimin' to take him a hunt fer Ol' Slewfoot. Well, they hain't nobody seed hair ner hide of him sinst. That was the evenin' afore you was tuck to the horspittle."

"Anybody been to look fer him?" Grannison asked, dreading the answer.

"Yeah, me an' Jeter here tuck a scoutin' trip up in thar a right smart ways. Didn't find nothin' though. We've figgered out he jest tuck a notion an' went off some'rs-back to Catalooch, like as not."

"I wouldn't be nary bit s'prised if he done that very thing," Grannison acquiesced readily.

Next morning Grannison started for the woods, alone. Against all reason he clung to an insane hope that Dugger might yet be alive. It would take a tough woodsman a long time to die with a broken leg. After an hour's labored climbing Cole had to stop for a breathing spell. He stood panting on a little rise where the sparser growth afforded a broken view in the direction of the fatal cliff. The sight

Courtesy of the Great Smoky Mountains National Park   Photographed by Edouard E. Exline

Huggins Hell from the Chimney Tops - 1937.

that met his eyes took the last remaining strength from his body. Wings. The very air was filled with wings. Broad, shadowy, slow-beating wings. Soaring, circling, settling down, rising again. Buzzard wings: obscene, loathsome, silent as death.

Dragging his sick body back to the cabin, Grannison took to his bed. Mat told him he looked like a skeer-crow that had been chased by a ha'nt. Short wintry days passed, dull and cheerless. Nights came and went, long, unrestful, fearsome with dreams of circling, swooping wings. December and January passed thus. February came.

The bear season neared its close, but no music of hounds had been heard in Huggins Hell. The neighbors had broached the matter more than once, but in strange fashion Grannison, to whom the chase had always been life itself, inveriably interposed some objection. "Too airly yit. The pelts won't be prime. The b'ars ain't fat. The dawgs ain't in shape—looks like ol' Duke's gittin the distemper."

"We ort to set some traps, anyhow," Uncle Nelse Walker urged. "Ye've allus had good luck trappin'."

"No!" thundered Grannison. "I'm through with trappin'. Don't intend to set nary another'n no time!"

That was "quare," Uncle Nelse thought. He talked to the Brackinses about it. "Might 'a' been owin' to that lick on the head back in the fall. A body can't tell. A pity, though, ain't it?"

It was "quare," too, about Sevier Dugger. What *had* happened to him? Had he ever really gone on that hunt he talked about? Somebody had heard a vague hint of foul play. Whispers of a quarrel. Grannison had uttered a threat. "Ye better let that b'ar-run alone. Remember I told ye!" Or something like that. Grannison's neighbors loyally pooh-poohed these rumors, caught over the grapevine telegraph.

"Nary word of truth in it. Grannison's rough, got a hot temper an' all that, but he wouldn't kill a man."

"He mought have had some words with Sevier about that hunt, but that was jest his way."

Anyhow, he ought to know of the talk that was going round. Newt and Zeke Brackins took it upon themselves to tell him. It didn't seem to disturb Grannison. He greeted it with a fair imitation of a laugh. Just the same, he made a trip to the county seat and secretly consulted a lawyer. When he came back he felt better. At least he looked better.

"Shucks!" he said indifferently to his cronies fore-gathered at Clegg's pounding-mill. "You-uns *know* I never killed Sevier Dugger. Fer the matter of that, who knows that Sevier's dead? Whar's the corpus delicti?"

"Whar's the which?" asked Zeke Brackins uncertainly.

"The corpus delicti. That means the corpse. They can't convict no man of a killin' less'n they perduce the corpus delicti. No corpse, no hangin'."

"Sounds reasonable," Zeke agreed.

"Hit's a law. An' they hain't perduced no corpus delicti fer Sevier Dugger, have they?"

The neighbors were reassured, but Grannison had another bad night. At daylight he rose, resolved to make another journey into the accursed Hell. He would gather up and bury all the bones the buzzards had scattered about. The trap, too. There would be no corpus delicti. Next day, though, it looked like rain. Besides, he wasn't feeling very chipper. But he would go tomorrow, sure.

The neighbors held another conclave at the pounding-mill. There was plenty of talk now. In Gatlinburg the tourists at the hotels were discussing it. An editorial in a Knoxville paper had demanded why the county officials didn't take action.

Courtesy of the Great Smoky Mountains National Park

Young hunter with his prey 1910 - 1920.

"Fellers," declared Uncle Nelse, "whilst I don't believe they'll ever pin nothin' on Grannison, they're like to cause him a heap of trouble."

"Yeah," agreed Newt Brackins, "an' all of us knows they's somethin' on his mind a-werryin' him."

"They's somethin' keeps him from ever goin' in the Hell any more," reasoned Jeter Clegg. "Maybe hit's that thar carpus elicti, er whatever hit is he calls hit."

"How about a bunch of us takin' a ja'nt in thar tomorrer an' seein' what we can see? We mought could help Grannison out if hit comes to court."

Next morning six veterans of the chase furtively entered the shadows of the Hell on the quest of they knew not what, but hoping only to bring into the sunlight some clue to the mystery that haunted and imperiled their comrade. And strangely enough, on that same day the High Sheriff, urged by the increasing clamor of the citizenry, rode into the Sugarlands. Cole, having waited one day too long to go and destroy the damning evidence the Hell concealed, heard the clink of horseshoes. But the hillsman did not turn a hair.

"Cole," the officer said quietly, "I guess you know what I've come for."

"No idy at all," drawled Grannison.

"I have a warrant charging you with the murder of one Sevier Dugger on or about the twentieth day of November last."

"All right, Sheriff," replied Cole without the flicker of a muscle. "I ain't guilty, but you've got yer duty. I'll go."

"That's sensible. Take time to arrange things so you can leave. I've an extra horse down at the bend."

Cole broke the news to Mat. Very calmly she rolled his extra clothes into a bundle, brought him a drink from the jug, and went to the spring for a bucket of water. While she was gone the two men heard voices. Out of the fringe of the Hell came six hunters. Two of them bore sacks across their shoulders. They filed silently into the yard, nodding incuriously at the sheriff.

"H'lo, Grannison."

"H'lo, boys. Whar you-uns been?"

"Up in the plumb middle of the Hell."

"Huntin'?"

"Ye mought call it that. Found somethin', anyhow."

One of the sacks was tossed upon the grass. From its mouth a pile of bones rolled partly out. In one hasty glance Grannison made out a thigh-bone, an arm, a section of vertebrae with ribs attached. Under the mountaineer's stubbly beard showed a greenish-gray pallor. This was the one thing he had feared. The terrible thing a mountain man most abhors and dreads. He had been "turned up." Swiftly the pallor turned to a red-hot flush of rage.

"Ye skunks! Ye devil-bred—"

"Keep yer shirt on, Grannison!" Zeke Brackins chuckled. "Here's somethin' else ye mought reckonize, too."

He tossed the second sack down. There was a rattling of metal and a chain lay on the ground alongside a rusty trap. The jaws of the trap still gripped a jagged end of bone, an ankle joint, some toes.

"Thar's the carpus elicti, I reckon," said Zeke dryly. " 'Lowed hit mought come in handy in court."

Grannison's nerve went to pieces like a shattered bowl. Betrayed! Informed against! Delivered to the gallows! And by these! His neighbors, his old cronies! Whimpering, sobbing like a whipped schoolboy, he turned to the officer.

"They've got me, Sheriff! I done it! But I never aimed to leave him thar to die. So he'p me, God, I didn't!"

"Grannison Cole," shouted Uncle Nelse, "have ye gone bodaciously crazy? Man, *take a look* at them bones!"

"No, no! I don't want to see 'em! Take 'em away!" Cole had slumped on the doorstep and hidden his face in his big hands.

"Gol durn ye, Grannison, don't act like a plumb lunatic! Look! Them ain't human bones!"

Slowly Grannison lifted his head. Then he let loose a yell that brought Mat from the spring house on the run.

"Why, I'll be durned! Why, them's a b'ar's bones!"

"Of course!" Newt chuckled. "That's what we was tryin' to show ye all the time. That's Ol' Slewfoot, cotched in yer own trap in the middle of the Hell!"

"Chaw my ears off if hit ain't!" roared the champeen. "Looky whar them two right front toes is missin!"

"Well, men," the sheriff interposed, "I don't know anything about this bear's skeleton, but I have to serve this warrant. Get ready, Cole."

"Bet yer life I'll go with ye, Sheriff!" bellowed Cole, now almost hysterical with laughter. "All the warrants in creation can't skeer me now!"

The officer and his prisoner were setting out on the long road to town when two lank hounds came sniffing out of the undergrowth on the edge of the Hell.

"Sevier Dugger's dawgs, or I'm a liar!" yelled Jeter Clegg excitedly.

"Yes, an' by jiminy, here comes Sevier hisself!" shouted Uncle Nelse Walker.

"Hit's him as shore as shootin'!" Clegg reiterated.

"Why, ye ol' son of a gun, Sevier, whar in time have ye been? We've ruck over Huggins Hell fer yer carcass, an' here ye turn up as lively an' as ornery as ye ever was!"

Dugger came up, grinning nonchalantly. Grannison Cole slid weakly from his saddle and leaned against the fence for support as Sevier narrated his adventures.

"You-uns recollect I was goin' out las' fall to bring in Ol' Slewfoot's hide. Well, when I got up thar to whar the new run starts, I found the ol' cuss cotched by his bad foot in a trap. I knowed then Grannison had the joke on me an' you-uns would devil me to death about it. So I up an' follered that run clear acrost into Ca'liny, to Catalooch, an' 'lowed I'd stay a spell."

"Didn't ye know hit was bein' norated ye'd been killed, an' they was layin' it to Grannison here?"

"Never heared it till yesterday, when a feller come in from this side an' told what they was rumorin'. I 'lowed then hit was time to come back an' straighten it out fer Grannison, an' here I am!"

Grannison Cole gazed at the returned Aeneas of the Sugarlands as if he were seeing a ghost. Then he extended a horny palm.

"Sevier, I done ye wrong. I sot that trap fer you. Then I come to my senses an' was startin' to git ye out, an' a tree fell on me an' busted my head. Ever sinst then I've been carryin' yer blood on my hands. Hit's nigh werried me to death, till I was wishin' they'd hang me an' git it over with."

He held on like a vise to Sevier's hand a long time before he could finish.

"Ey Gad, but I'm glad to see ye back—ye dad-gummed ol' corpus delicti!"

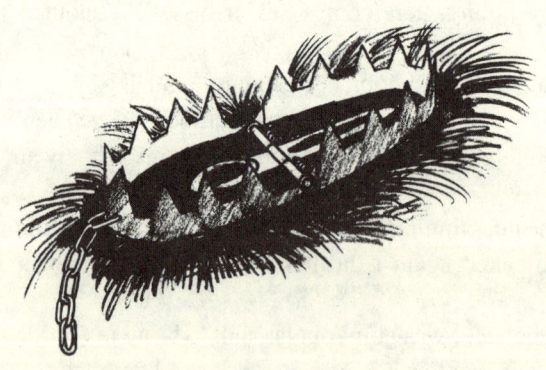

WILLOW PATTERN

This tale starts with a lump of mud. Not just common everyday mud, though; for the English hillside it came from furnished the clay that made the potteries of Staffordshire famous a century and a half ago. Furthermore, this particular lump, by decree of a kindly destiny, was thrown upon the wheel of one Josiah Spode—the Second Josiah Spode. And when he had fashioned it and stamped his letter "S" upon it, it was no longer a lump of mud, but a blue underglaze platter in the famous "willow pattern" that all lovers of old English pottery know and admire.

How this Spode willow pattern came at long last to be the most cherished heirloom in the colonial farmhouse of John Hendrix in Tidewater, Virginia, might well be a colorful yarn in itself, but it is here merely mentioned as a bit of background; because our story really begins on the day when Mrs. John Hendrix discovered that the precious Spode was missing.

It was a queer piece of business, and Mrs. Hendrix was quite upset about it. Apparently the platter had just walked out of its rack in the Domestic Arts booth at the county fair. And with its blue ribbon, too, which the judges had attached when they awarded it the first prize in the silver and china display. Now deep down inside, Lou Hendrix couldn't help feeling that Mrs. Serena Simerly, who had had charge of the booth, ought to have been more watchful. She couldn't come out and say so, of course; the two families living on adjoining farms and Serena such a good neighbor, and all. Serena herself was in a state of consternation.

"Oh, Lou, I'm just sick about it!" she lamented after both women had searched through the booth for the third time. "And I'd tried to be so careful of everything!"

"No use to worry over it now," said Lou resignedly. "You had your hands full with such crowds around all the time and people handling the exhibits and asking all kinds of questions."

"But when I think how hard I begged you to enter it, Lou—I was just so sure it would win a first—"

"Well, I oughtn't to have consented to the entry. You see, it's John's—came down from his great-grandmother back in England, and he'd rather lose the farm than that dish. He's always said he was going to give it to Van and his bride on their wedding day. He's talked about it a hundred times, I guess."

"Yes, my dear, and that's what makes me feel all the more wretched about it. But I'm not going to give up. It's bound to turn up in a day or two. Somebody's just taken it out by mistake."

"No, Serena, I don't expect ever to see it again. We'll let it go and forget about it. John—he was almost furious when he found I'd let it out of the house—wouldn't go about the Domestic Arts exhibits. I'll bet he doesn't even know it took the prize."

It taxed Lou's wifely diplomacy through the days that followed to steer the family conversation away from the delicate subject of the lost platter. Fortunately, there was much else to talk about. Lou had won her full quota of blue, red, or green ribbons on needlework, fancy eggs, and cold-pack vegetables in glass, and John's own winnings on expertly graded bright-leaf tobacco "hands" had been written up on the first page of the county papers. One way or another, though, Lou had managed to avoid any questioning about the Spode.

"I'll just let him think it's where it's always been kept, in the dining room cupboard, and he may never bother to look for it or ask about it," she told herself. "And some day, when I'm in the city, I'll find a match for it in an antique shop, if it takes a year's egg money."

One thing that helped to drive the incident out of mind was the not unexpected announcement of the engagement of Van Hendrix and Flo Simerly. Lou and Serena, each with motherly understanding, had watched the youngsters grow up from tiny tads sliding down strawstacks, fishing for minnows in the creek, and fleeing with screams from hissing ganders in the spring-lot. And now, noting that the old cow path across the intervening pasture field was smoother-worn than it had been before, the mothers smiled. For it was the most natural thing in the world.

If only Lou could have put the thought of the platter out of mind as she really tried to do; and if, and if— But despite herself the mystery of the thing would keep coming back to her. Certainly careless of Serena. Lou couldn't feel otherwise about it. And Serena had been so persistent about having it. She'd made three trips across the pasture before Lou would agree to let it go.

"Queer, too, how daffy Serena's always been about that Spode," Lou would muse as she did her morning work. "She's told me so often about the fire that burned her father's house when she was a girl and destroyed all the china and things that were to have been hers."

Then Lou would feel ashamed of herself for brooding over the matter—she oughtn't ever to think of it again. But she would.

"Something fishy, the way she always had to have a look at it whenever she dropped in. And that time she borrowed it when a lot of company came—and kept it six months, till I had to ask her for it."

So, unbidden, came the sheeted ghost of unneighborly suspicion to walk the clover and tobacco fields under a Virginia moon. Not for the world, though, would Lou have pointed a finger of accusation. It was only her ever-present dread of John's disappointment and disapproval when he should know, as sooner or later he must know. Lou grew jittery every time she thought of that. It was strange, she knew, that a cool-headed, even-tempered, considerate man like John should be so set up in a piece of crockery. But Lou knew John. She *thought* she knew Van, too. But who does know a boy in love?

"Say, Momsie," Van inquired casually, rummaging through the cupboard for a piece of pie to sustain life between "quittin' time" and supper time, "where's Dad's big blue dish you used to keep on this shelf?"

Lou's face paled. John was reading the paper on the front porch.

"Sh! Don't shout so, son. Why, let me see—I don't remember just now. Why do you ask?"

"Oh, no reason at all. Just hadn't noticed it lately—not since the fair, I guess."

Then the gray ghost, or something, must have waved a shadowy hand before Lou's troubled eyes. Unknown to herself, all the pent-up wonderings and petulant musings of the past weeks lent a bitterness to her tone.

"Nobody else has, if you want to know—unless it's your future mother-in-law. But for heaven's sake don't breath a word of it to your father."

Courtesy of the Great Smoky Mountains National Park   Photographed by Maurice Sullivan

Making lye soap - 1935. Notice the hawk's wing fan in the young woman's hand.

But the insinuation in her words was lost upon literal-minded, unsuspicious Van. That very evening as he sat with Flo in the moonlight on the Simerly veranda, he suddenly thought of something.

"By the way, sweetheart, I understood Moms to say your mother has that old Spode platter of hers. If she's through with it I'll just take it with me when I go."

It was midsummer, but for the rest of the evening there seemed to be a cloud over the moon and a peculiar chill in the evening air. Next day's mail brought a crisp note from Flo—with a ring enclosed. And the path across the pasture began from that day to fade out, overgrown with grass and weeds. Which also was the most natural thing in the world, but for both Van and Flo the most terrible thing that ever happened.

Van took it with tight-set lips and stiffened jaw. And remembering what his mother had said about keeping the thing from his father, he said nothing. All John observed was that the boy didn't shave and dress every evening after work was over, and that he was a demon for farm labor. Through the tobacco-cutting season he drove four good horses to gauntness, half a dozen tenants to distraction, and his own stalwart frame to a skeleton. Lou had been horrified when Van naively confessed to blurting out her unguarded insinuation to Flo. But now that the fat was in the fire she sought outspokenly to justify herself.

"Of course, son, I never dreamed of your mentioning it, and I'm awfully sorry for the mess it's stirred up, but, after all, I can't help believing she took that platter. Why, if her conscience had been clear she wouldn't have flared up so."

"But, Momsie, it was such a trifle to break up a family friendship over—to say nothing of Flo and me. What did we have to do with the darned old dish, anyhow?" Van argued glumly.

"I'm so sorry, son," answered Lou, repentant. "But I was all torn up, and am yet, dreading the time when your father finds out about it. It was the first time I ever went squarely against his wishes."

"Oh, well, we'll drop it. But I wish the confounded old plate had stayed back in England." With that he took his battered hat and went to the field.

As for Flo, she had started off bravely enough, singing snatches of sprightly college songs as she rattled the dishes in the sink. Loyally she boiled with rage at the deliberate insult to her mother.

"If he thinks his mother can call you a common sneak thief and get away with it," she stormed, "he's a yellow hound—and I don't want ever to see him again!"

Before many days, though, Serena noted that whenever the Hendrix farm wagon clattered down the turnpike Flo's eyes would be furtively peering through the half-closed shades at the slumping figure in the driver's seat, and then the girl would take to her bed for the rest of the day.

"Poor child, it's killing her!" Serena would tell herself reproachfully, and the pain of it would make the sting of the unjust accusation against herself seem slight in comparison.

"Why did I take it so seriously?" she groaned. "If I'd just laughed it off as a joke. But now everything's ruined past all mending."

Week after week Serena saw her own flesh and blood pining, paling to a shadow. Flo wouldn't let her even mention the subject or anything connected with it. But the mother's sleep was broken nightly by two haunting pictures: Flo's wan face at a darkened window, and a great oval dish with oriental willow-fronds showering tears into a river spanned by an arching bridge—and two mourning doves perched desolately above the treetops.

Lou Hendrix made her semi-annual shopping pilgrimage to the big city. Her rounds of the department stores and the five-and-tens completed, she dropped into an antique shop.

"I'd like to see some English chinaware, especially some platters in the willow pattern, if you've anything in stock."

"I believe we have," the saleswoman replied obligingly, "Step this way, please."

There were several willow platters, mostly good reproductions, but two were flawless originals, bearing the unmistakable "S" of Josiah Spode the Second.

"I want something to replace one that's been in the family for generations—and that—got lost," Lou explained. "This one here is almost a perfect match—size, coloring, and everything. Only mine had a tiny nick here on the rim, just above the two doves."

"Well, madam, if you want a perfect matching, our retouching department can easily mark it exactly like the original."

That night Lou Hendrix, for all she'd had to forego the purchase of a living room rug she'd wanted a long time, slept more soundly than she had done for months. But John would never know why. To be sure, only one of the two heavy burdens on her heart had been lifted, she realized with sadness. Her heart still ached every time she saw Van, unshaven, haggard, going about his tasks like the most spiritless hired hand.

And Serena Simerly, seeing for the hundredth time the pitiful figure of Flo weeping her heart out on her bed felt like a murderess.

"It's all my fault!" she moaned. "After all, it *was* my carelessness that caused the whole wretched business. How can I blame Lou for feeling as she does? It's going to drive me stark mad!"

She tried to read, but the printed page was meaningless.

"*I must do something!* I'm willing to face any rebuff, any humiliation, if only I can patch up our broken friendship and put things back where they were for Flo and Van!"

The longer she brooded the more fantastic and unreal the thing became, and the less her own wound rankled. She came to feel a sense of self-condemnation, to see herself through Lou's eyes, recreant to a trust, unfair, dishonest.

"Why *shouldn't* she think of me so? The plate was hers. I teased her into lending it. I lost it. I might as well have stolen it. In a sense I *did* steal it! . . . And I'm going to give it back!"

A few days later Serena walked into the antique shop in the city and asked to see some willow pattern plates. The clerk brought out the collection, including the one remaining original Spode.

"This is just what I'm looking for," Serena said. "I want it to replace one I—let get away."

"We frequently have calls like that, for such pieces as this especially. Were there any flaws or marks on the original you'd like to have reproduced?"

"I hardly remember. Seems, though, there *was* a very small nicked place somewhere on the rim, but I couldn't just describe it."

"Probably a surface chipping—say about here?" the clerk suggested smilingly. "That can be handled without a bit of trouble. We do it every week."

Next afternoon Serena slipped out at the back gate and picked her way along the grass-grown path. Lou Hendrix received her with embarrassed politeness. Serena was first to speak.

"Lou," she began calmly, "I've come on a strange errand. It's taken months to make me see it's the only thing to do. I've brought home your Spode platter."

"Why, Serena," Lou exclaimed, "you mean that someone found it and returned it to you?"

"I do not. No one else had anything to do with it."

"But I don't understand. And, Serena, I want to tell you now that I could have bitten my tongue out a million times for hinting to Van that I thought you'd been careless about looking after it."

"I wasn't careless, Lou," Serena lied, though in her overwrought state she made herself believe she was telling a hideous, damning truth. "I always envied you that platter. I wanted it. I took it. And it's nearly driven me insane. It's wrecked our children's lives. Now I'm begging you to take it back—and to forgive me!"

She hid her face in her apron, sobbing hysterically. Lou, too, was crying unabashed.

"Oh, my dear, I'll never believe for one instant that you deliberately took it—I can understand. But if it will make you feel better, and if it will help us to fix things up again for the children, I'll take it."

The two women dried their eyes and clasped each other's hands in pledge of the old friendship renewed in the burning baptism of tears. Then they worked out a plan to explain matters to Van and Flo, involving neither accusation nor confession, but smoothing all differences, wiping out all ill-feeling.

"Whatever shall I do with two Spodes?" Lou asked herself in bewilderment. "I don't suppose the antique dealer would take one back. And John must never see but one. Funny, he's never even suspected the old one wasn't in its place all the time. But I wouldn't go through the nightmare of this thing again for all the china in the world!"

Thereafter one Spode, the one Serena had brought, reposed in the familiar corner of the cupboard. The other was carefully hidden in the linen closet, under the best tablecloths. No man ever set foot in that sanctum.

Meanwhile Lou and Serena's strategy worked, albeit not without a deal of diplomacy and a tearful seance of questioning on Flo's part. But the blessed sight of the two mothers visiting each other again, chatting and bantering in the old friendly way, healed the scars of estrangement. And the sun shone brighter by day, the moon beamed more softly through the apple trees at night. The wedding took place just after Christmas and was followed by a dinner at John and Lou's house.

Aunt Roxie, who had reigned as queen of the Hendrix kitchen for thirty years, laid down the law to her mistress. "Now, Mis' Lou, yo' ain' gonna set foot in de kitchen dis day! Yo-all got a-plenty to do 'thout werryin' ovah no dinnah fixin's."

"All right, Roxie," laughed Lou. "I know the dinner's in good hands, and I'll obey orders."

The bridal party sat down to Roxie's culinary masterpiece, and the hostess took an appraising and approving look at the perfectly appointed table. In the full pride of her two hundred pounds of ebony dignity entered Roxie, bearing aloft the steaming turkey, and followed by her daughter, as second waitress, carrying the great golden Virginia baked ham. Lou glanced casually at the two platters, one at the head, the other at the foot of the table—and her heart stopped. Roxie had found the other Spode!

Lou's crimson blush of mortification went unnoticed, though, for at that moment John Hendrix rose in his place to greet his guests in true Southern wedding feast style.

"Friends, before we proceed to partake of this modest repast, I wish to greet you one and all and bid you welcome to the happy occasion. And in honor of this occasion I desire to bestow upon my new daughter and her fortunate husband a token of my fatherly regard and affection; something that I've kept and prized through the years for just this day and this hour."

He unwrapped a package he had placed beside his chair.

"My great-grandmother's old English dinner platter!"

As the applause died away John glanced down at the turkey, which awaited his practiced carving hand, and for the first time saw the dish upon which it lay. He laughed.

"Why, Mother, I thought you knew what I planned—to have Roxie take the turkey back and exchange platters. And here you've gone and borrowed one! All my fault. I might as well confess. When this plate went to the fair last fall I got uneasy about it, and slipped it out while Mrs. Simerly was busy at the other end of the booth. And for fear Mother would be lending it again to some church bazaar or something, I tucked it away in the bottom of that old trunk of mine in the attic."

Flo and Van stared in wonderment. Lou and Serena exchanged one glance. In that glance the whole drama moved swiftly to the denouement. Was it stark tragedy—cruel, false accusation—self-immolation, the pain, the pity of the past months? It might have been. But this was no time nor place for tragedy or heartbreak.

So the two women, with a wisdom that only mothers have, did just the right thing. They laughed. Then the bride and the groom laughed, too. That's what wedding dinners are for. The guests laughed, though a bit mystified as to what the joke was. John Hendrix laughed, beaming upon them all as a jovial host should do. Aunt Roxie laughed, shaking her fat sides until her apronstring burst.

At the sound of that laughter the gray ghost that had shadowed the masterpiece of Josiah Spode the Second went slinking back to the old churchyard in Staffordshire, and three pairs of cooing doves hovered amorously above the willow tops.

SHAKE RAG SHOWS 'EM

The serpent of modernism had reared its scaly head in the erstwhile peaceful settlement of Shake Rag, and Preachin' Jake Buckner felt himself ordained to scotch the reptile. It all began when the teacher of "Home Ec" in the backwoods high school introduced a daring innovation into the education program of the mountain hamlet by organizing a girls' basketball team. The girls, needless to say, had taken to the idea with all the zest of the healthy young beings they were, but parental enthusiasm was sadly wanting. Within a week a group of patrons had started an opposition party and Preachin' Jake was its noisy spokesman.

His first skirmish was with his own fair and strapping daughter Flossie, who had announced at the supper table her election as captain of the team.

"Now looky here, they ain't nary bit of sense in a passel of grown gals a-playin' ball like boys," her reverend father asserted sternly. "I'm sendin' ye to school to larn yer books, not to be frolickin' around like a jack rabbit."

"But, Pap," the girl argued, "Miss Tyler says we need to study some and play some, and she 'lows basketball is good healthy exercise."

"Healthy!" Jake snorted in disgust. "What does a gal like you keer about bein' any more healthier than she is? Ye're as strong as a mule an' never had a sick day in yer life. If ye're sp'ilin' fer exercise ye can walk home an' tote firewood, slop the hawgs, milk the cow-brute, an' help yer mammy in the kitchen."

"But, Pap," Flossie persisted, "Miss Tyler says all up-to-date schools has athletics. Hit makes the students study their lessons harder after they play a while."

"Shucks!" The austere keeper of the public conscience banged the table until the dishes clattered. "D'ye reckon us taxpayers is diggin' down in our jeans to run a neighborhood playhouse? Hit's jist another fandangle these town folks has thought up—puny wimmin folks that never in life done an honest day's work in the cornfield or the tater patch."

After this mild fashion the argument started, and it waxed hotter and more vehement. Preachin' Jake Buckner was a power in speech. The mountain folk said he was the rantin'est, roarin'est, rousin'est preacher in five counties. When he turned loose his vials of wrath against the Devil and his cohorts you could almost see the grass wither, the leaves curl with the heat, and human souls fry in blue blazes.

Flossie, however, was a worthy daughter of such a sire. She stood five-eleven in her sturdy bare feet, and in her nineteen years had worked many a grown man to a standstill with axe, hoe, or brier-scythe. As for nerve, there wasn't a created thing, biped, quadruped, reptile, or other varmint she had ever been "skeered of,"—not even Preachin' Jake himself.

Consequently, when her father's characteristic outburst had spent itself, Flossie went back to school with his grudging permission to keep on playing basketball provided she should always get home in time to help with the chores and should spend her Saturdays in the field.

The team developed steadily under Miss Tyler's expert coaching and Flossie's vigorous captaincy. And such a team! Mountain girls every one, tall, brawny, deep-chested, hard-muscled, tough-winded. They worked hard and responded intelligently. Their chief defect was lack of speed and agility. But they were dogged and determined and the coach surveyed her work with growing pride.

Shake Rag had no gymnasium, and the new sport had to be staged on the gravel of the school yard, between the wooden goal posts that supported the homemade basket rings. The problem of costumes was temporarily solved by Miss Tyler's ingenuity and the willing fingers of the Home Ec girls, which transformed faded print dresses into somewhat baggy bloomers and blouses. Rubber-soled "sneakers"—boy's sizes—served for gym shoes, though most of the team, accustomed to hoeing corn barefoot in traditional mountain fashion, usually spared their feet the unwonted confinement and made the loose pebbles fly with their unsandaled soles.

The first practice games drew regular circus crowds. The whole countryside seemed to have urgent business in Shake Rag. The Reverend Jake came once, quite by accident, he explained, had one eye-filling look, and blew up like a rusty boiler.

"Lord 'a' mercy, folks!" he exclaimed in horror to the little group of the faithful, congregated in front of Silas Golloway's crossroads store. "Them young wimmen is paradin' around in the midst of a crowd of men an' boys with nothin' on but a shirt an' a shift, an' nary a sign of a stockin' on their limbs! Hit ain't decent. Any gal that gits out in a public place that away, a-kickin' up her heels an' cavortin' like a calf, is prancin' down the broad road to deestruction! I'm goin' to take my gal out an' keep her out!"

"Amen! Ye're right, Preacher!" the storekeeper echoed. "My Ann's in it too, but this is her last day. Hit jist won't never do!"

Despite these dire threats and prohibitions, however, the new sport flourished apace and the fame of the husky team, the Shake Rag Boomers, spread into the darkest hollows of the scattered settlement. And Flossie Buckner and Ann Golloway, as "center" and "left forward" respectively, continued to be the brightest stars in its all-star cast.

Preachin' Jake's crusade for the decorous concealment of the female "limb" had nevertheless aroused such a widespread protest against the "shirt and shift" that Miss Tyler had felt constrained to offer a compromise. From that day forward the girls practiced in black cotton stockings, and over their bloomers they wore wide skirts that fell below their knees.

Through the long autumn afternoons the girls practiced diligently. They became less clumsy in their dodging and pivoting. Their passing, dribbling, juggling, and shooting took on a semblance of system and training.

Meanwhile the popular curiosity became less avid, the crowds of spectators smaller. By Thanksgiving Day basketball had been accepted as a part of the established scheme of things. But the zeal of the players never abated. Even on raw wintry days the hardy maidens, inured to cold and damp, often insisted on playing, though their coach shivered in a heavy sweater and coat.

Quite unexpectedly Miss Tyler received a letter from the manager of the Brownsboro High School team inviting the Shake Rag Boomers to come to the city for a December game. Since the Brownsboro "Brownies" were reputed the best team in the county association, Miss Tyler hesitated before accepting the challenge. She finally laid the question before her team.

"Now, girls, we'd have to remember that this would be just a practice game for the Brownies. They have a fine gym and a fast team picked from three hundred girls. They've played for years and expect to win the county cup again this season. But if you're willing to work your hardest and give them your best we'll sign up for the date."

"Whatever Floss says will be all right with me," Ann Golloway said after a moment's silence had fallen on the group.

"If hit's for me to say, then we go," replied Flossie, lapsing into the patois of the cove-country, as she usually did when she wasn't in an English class. "Those girls ain't any bigger than we are, I reckon. Anyhow, we ain't skeered to go agin' nobody."

"Fine! Then of course we go!" declared Miss Tyler. "Flossie has the right idea even if her grammar does slip a bit! But, girls," the coach added more seriously, "if we make this trip we simply must have regulation basketball suits. These homemade things are all right to practice in, but when we go to the city we're going to look as smart as the Brownies. The question is, how can we raise the money?"

That brought on more talk and sundry plans were suggested—none of which, for obvious reasons, involved asking the girls' fathers for the money. Instead it was agreed unanimously that this bit of financing was to be a strictly personal and private matter.

"I think I know how I can get mine," Flossie volunteered. "Pap said last night he was goin' to have to hire a man to grub the sassafras an' mow the blackberry briers out of the new ground so he can put it in corn in the spring. I can do it in two Saturdays an' I guess he'd as soon pay me as anybody."

Well, one way or another, the money was soon raised and the suits were ordered. There was little time to spare, for mails to and from Shake Rag are both slow and uncertain. The Boomers and their instructor were therefore on tenterhooks for a whole week, fearing they might have to invade the county metropolis in their calico rags.

In fact, the precious package did arrive by the very last mail before the team climbed into the "mountain schooner" for the first lap of the tiresome journey. As the lumbering wagon bumped over the rocky road down the shadowy meanderings of Thunderin' Creek, the girls tore the wrappings from the package and examined the new toggery with an inward excitement that their native stoicism but partially concealed.

The twenty-mile wagon ride brought the Boomers to the turnpike, where they boarded a bus for Brownsboro. At dusk, the bus driver set them down at their hotel, just as the electric lights began to blaze along the little city's "white way." It was the first time any of the girls had ever seen so large a town. After a light supper they reveled in the novelty of a trolley ride to the High School, ten blocks across the city.

The scene in the dressing-room of the gymnasium was an exciting episode in an eventful day. The new suits were of the newest design, entirely sleeveless, almost backless, and with decidedly rudimentary trunks. The husky lassies from the hills certainly filled them snugly.

"Good gracious, Miss Tyler, is this all of it?" Phenie McMasters asked in astonishment as she surveyed herself in the big mirror.

"There's enough, isn't there?" replied the coach smilingly.

"I guess so. These town folks may be used to this kind of clothes, but they'll sure turn Shake Rag pop-eyed when we get home!"

"Say!" exclaimed Ann Golloway panic-stricken. "My dad and some other men at the store said they might take a notion to come down on the late bus and see the game!"

"Oh, *if* they do!" groaned Liz McKinney. "We'll never get to go nowhere agin nor see nothin'."

"I ain't much skeered that Pap will come," remarked Flossie Buckner with a shrug. "But if he does, I'm sunk! And after two Saturdays of grubbin' in that new ground, too! Believe me, I *worked* for these doll clothes. The briers tore might' nigh every rag off o' me, an' most of my hide, too!"

"You don't need to tell *us* about the hide, Floss," said Ann with a glance at her captain's sturdy framework. "You look like somebody had drawn a map of Great Smoky on your underpinning!"

Truth to tell, Flossie was a bit conspicuous in more ways than one. Her suit, to begin with, was a trifle more than snug-fitting. Her muscular calves were golden brown with a tan only sun, wind, and rain on a hillside cornfield can produce, but they still bore witness to those two recent Saturdays in the new ground. Both legs were criss-crossed with innumerable red scratches that would need several weeks for nature to erase. Flossie had surely earned the price of her striking regalia!

"I know I look like a skinned mule," she chuckled as she gave her team mates a final word of counsel. "But, girls, we came down here to play basketball, not to put on a beauty show. We're going to forget looks and keep our blinkers on the ball. And if any of our dads are up there in those seats they'll have to look out for their own eyesight!"

At ten minutes before eight both teams emerged from their dressing rooms with a hop-skip-and-jump and began to warm up, to the accompaniment of a deafening din led by the school band. The Brownie sextet, a fast aggregation of trim, wiry city lassies, sailed instantly into the preliminary practice, circling with almost dizzy speed in a series of well-timed passes from center to goal, each forward as she passed under the basket deftly tossing the ball in a graceful arc and seldom missing a shot.

The girls from the mountains, dazed by the brilliant floodlight, the blare of the music, and the up-roarious yells from the galleries, were some minutes in finding themselves. They were out of their element, like a team of plow horses before a grandstand on a Derby race track.

With the native self-possession of mountain youngsters, however, they rallied after a bit and remembered what they had come thither to do. Considering their newness and rawness they made a fairly creditable showing in the practice work. No doubt the new suits helped materially both ways, improving the team's appearance and strengthening its morale.

"Gee, Floss!" Ann Golloway whispered as the two paused a moment for breath. "Just s'pose these suits hadn't come. Wouldn't we 'a' looked like somethin' from the big woods!"

"Ain't it so!" the tall captain agreed. "Ours are just like those the Brownies are wearin'—only a wee bit shorter. They're fightin' clothes, and don't you fergit it!"

At that instant, though, her eyes opened wide with astonishment as her gaze roamed upward to the spectators' seats.

"Lord help us, Ann!" she gasped. "There's Pap sittin' up there, an' your dad right beside him. Yes, an' the whole Shake Rag bunch. Pap looks like he was gazin' straight into the mouth of Hell, his eyes bulgin' out an' his jaw droppin'. But somehow I'm not afeared of him nor the town girls, nor the Devil himself tonight!"

Sure enough, Preachin' Jake, Silas Golloway, and a dozen other patrons of the seat of learning on Thunderin' Creek had followed the team to the city and were ensconced in the gallery. Jake Buckner had at first scorned the idea of making the trip, deeming it beneath the dignity of his high calling to patronize a place of worldly amusement. On second thought, however, he had decided that it might be his duty to go. Towns and cities he reckoned to be the Devil's own haunts and the centers of wickedness. The perils that might beset a group of innocent maidens in such a place were grave enough to necessitate his personal presence. Besides, he ought to see for himself, just once, a few of the awful goings-on he had so often and so stoutly thundered against from his pulpit.

His worst suspicions were fully confirmed when his eyes fell upon the Brownsboro players prancing out upon the court. He had chanced to see them first, inasmuch as he was sitting nearer the home team's goal.

"Lord 'a' mercy!" was his horrified exclamation. "I've heard about sich, but I never 'lowed I'd live to see the like with my own eyes! I'm thankful we made our gals wear clo'es that's anyhow half'way respectable!"

But at that moment he turned toward the opposite goal and his breath almost stopped. He didn't recognize the Shake Rag girls for a fraction of a minute, though, and was about to conclude there had been a change of the schedule. Then Flossie strode forth at the head of the circling column of the Shake Rag Boomers, and there was no mistaking Flossie. In the same instant five of his neighbors recognized each his own offspring under the blazing electric lights.

"That the shame of thy nekkedness do not appear," Jake quoted solemnly the words of a text he had more than once used to point a scathing rebuke against the unblushing scantiness of female apparel in this degenerate age. "I ortn't to 'a' come. Hit ain't no place fer a minister of the gospel!"

"Ye're right, Preacher!" Silas Golloway agreed fervently. "What d'ye say to gittin' out o' here, away from these scand'lous doin's?"

"No, bein' as I'm here I 'low I'll stay. But wait till we git them gals an' that thar teacher woman back home!"

The whistle blew and the teams lined up for the initial toss. Flossie Buckner, playing center for the Boomers, towered a full eight inches above her Brownie opponent. The city girl, though, seemed mounted on springs as she shot upward to slap the ball in mid-air. But Flossie scarcely rising on tiptoe, thrust aloft her long right arm and pushed the ball into Ann Golloway's waiting hands.

The Brownie who guarded Ann was a short girl, but seemingly made of India rubber. Ann could easily have pitched her over the railing into the stands, but she couldn't get away from her. Unused to such lightning-quick guarding, Ann tried in vain to pivot but fumbled and lost the ball to her opponent. Within twenty seconds it had progressed by a perfectly executed series of feints and passes to the Brownie's right forward, who made a clean shot for the goal. The yellow sphere dropped through the basket rim, and a white numeral "two" flashed upon the scoreboard.

That was the inauspicious start of Shake Rag's debut upon the arena of interscholastic sport. It left the Boomers dazed by the suddenness of it. The Brownsboro fans went wild, scenting easy victory and a fat score.

It was the old story of science and skill matched against main strength and awkwardness. The mountain girls were taller, heavier, and stronger, but the town youngsters were quicker, better trained, and cocksure of themselves. Besides, the Boomers had a bad attack of stage fright. They seemed to have forgotten everything Miss Tyler had ever taught them. Before the first half ended they had drawn nearly every penalty prescribed in the rule book. They held, shoved, tripped, charged, and double dribbled. The city girls spent half their time making free throws from the foul line.

Nevertheless, the visiting team managed to score an occasional field goal. These shots were greeted by groans and catcalls from the fans, and by grim silence in the little band of hillsmen. That silence was owing in part to the mountain men's total ignorance of the game. To them it was only mad, meaningless jumping about on the part of a dozen utterly crazy and most improperly clad young women. The wild cheering in the stands was equally senseless. Preachin' Jake and his scandalized compatriots could see no more point in the organized yells and songs and the synchronized exhortation to "Fight 'em, team! Fight 'em!" than they could in the exhibition of lunacy on the playing floor below.

Before long, however, they discovered that there was a certain relationship between the playing and the cheering. It also grew clear that the players' interest was centered in causing the ball to fall through the rim of a suspended fish net; and that the six city girls were doing this rather more often than their antagonists.

To the men from the cove the most impressive part of the whole performance was the role played by the cheerleader in the grandstand. He was a plump, cherub-faced, pink-cheeked, sleek-haired Fauntleroy of seventeen in gaily beribboned jersey and immaculate white duck trousers.

This youthful choragus, Herbie Wilson by name, was indebted to nature chiefly for his softly rotund figure and a high-pitched treble voice of remarkable penetrating power. To art he owed the enhancement of his beauty through the diligent efforts of the local masseurs and manicurists, and the amplification of his vocal powers by means of a huge cardboard megaphone. And with what both nature and art had done Herbie was completely satisfied.

Although the game had started out to be a runaway for Brownsboro, the Boomers had gradually begun to find themselves, and their end of the score began creeping up. At the end of the half the board showed twenty-six to twelve in Brownsboro's favor, but the Brownies were tiring while the Boomers were just getting their second wind.

Between halves a group of ardent fans, sipping their sodas in the lower corridor, held a council of war.

"I tell yuh," Herbie Wilson declared oracularly, "those big stiffs are slow as Christmas but they're as strong as mules, and this game ain't won yet!"

"You said it Herbie," a nervous, excited senior girl broke in, her voice between a whisper and a croak. "They were scared to death at first, but they're getting over it. We've got to rag 'em and rattle 'em. Herbie, you've got to give 'em the works!"

"That's the dope," Herbie agreed. "Leave 'em to me. We're goin' after 'em hard, especially that big center. She's half the team anyhow. I wish I knew her name."

"It's Flossie somebody," two or three volunteered.

"Right-o!" chortled Herbie. "We'll give Miss Flossie the raspberry from now on!"

As the teams resumed their positions for the second half the shrill voice of the cheerleader rose above the clamor. "Hey, Flossie! My! How yuh've grown since we saw yuh last!"

This opening sally was greeted with uproarious laughter, but if the visiting center noticed it she gave no sign.

Again Herbie's megaphone shrilled out over the tumult. "Say, folks, meet Flossie, the moon fixer from the tall timber!" This effort had put a heavy strain upon Herbie's inventive faculties, but the effect fully justified the intellectual energy expended. The deafening roar that followed it was possibly responsible for two more fouls which the referee chalked up against the Boomers.

"Step up, good people, and see the female giant from Smoky!" Herbie sang out once more. "She's been twice around the world with Barnum and Bailey. The tallest specimen in captivity!"

This one so taxed its author's resources that he had to rest for some minutes thereafter. Meanwhile the Brownies scored two more field goals, but the slow, steady machine from Shake Rag countered with four, the last a long shot from center by "the female giant from Smoky."

Herbie racked his brain once more. "Careful, Flossie! When you jump like that you may bump your head on the rafters!"

That wasn't so good, as the pink he-doll himself realized. Flossie responded by placing two more spectacular shots. Herbie's head was beginning to ache from the intensity of his cerebral exertions. Then some kindly muse must have whispered in his ear.

"Hey, Flossie!" he began. "No, I mean Bossie! Hey, Bossie, old cow!"

This outburst of genius swept the stands from one end to the other. Five hundred jubilant voices took up the cue. "Hey Bossie! Soo, Bossie! Soo-oo-oo, Bossie! Soo-oo-oo, cow!"

No doubt about that one. It was perfect, and the tremendous acclaim it won was ambrosia and nectar to Herbie's hungry pride. Flossie's face went suddenly white, a ghastly white under the thick tan. She fumbled, lost an easy shot; whereupon the din broke out again.

Then the girl's pallor vanished and a crimson flush rose in her cheeks. Preachin' Jake from his seat observed her reaction and understood. He himself had been first amused, then embarrassed, by the singling out of his daughter for the hilarity of the crowd. He spoke quietly to Silas Golloway.

"That young feller with the dinner horn is makin' a mistake. He figgered on pesterin' Floss an' gittin' her deviled so she can't play good. That's all right. But when he called her a cow he went a smidgin' too fur. He's got her mad now, an' hit don't do nobody no good to make Floss mad."

Preachin' Jake had unconsciously become absorbed in the game. With native shrewdness he had figured out a good deal of the strategy in the contest. He saw that his girl and his neighbors' girls were fighting against heavy odds but with a slim chance of victory.

As for Flossie, she was in that fight now, every inch and every ounce of her. She was everywhere on the floor, lips tight, teeth set, eyes always on the flying ball. And the score was a tie, with two minutes left to play.

Herbie Wilson now launched his last frantic attack upon Flossie. "Poor old Bossie! The dogs have been chasing her through the briers. Just look at the scratches on her!"

The crowd yelled its delight. Spectators held their sides and tears rolled down laughing faces. The Boomers had dropped to the floor at the "time out" signal and calmly surveyed the mad scene above. Someone asked, "Why, where did Floss go?"

Her place in the circle was empty. Two seconds later a dramatic hush fell upon the crowd. Something was happening, unheard of in the annals of basketball. The statuesque figure of the visitors' captain had entered the grandstand from somewhere and was moving swiftly on noiseless feet to the center of the lowest tier of seats, stopping just in front of the cheerleader and the bevy of his female admirers.

Snatching the megaphone from his chubby hand she placed it to her own lips. There issued a long-drawn, deep-toned call, the distressful lowing of a cow. It was the alarm cry of a distracted bovine mother, far more realistic than Herbie's powers of mimicry could have achieved. Then Flossie's own voice rang through the astonished silence.

"Yes, folks, ol' Bossie's been in the brier patch, but hit wasn't the dogs a-chasin' her. She was huntin' her calf—her nice fat baby bull calf that was lost. An' now she's found him! You've heared him bleatin' an' bellerin' here tonight, like a critter that was bein' weaned. Ol' Boss is goin' to give him somethin' to beller for!"

Turning swiftly she brought the megaphone down with a bang, crushing it upon Herbie's pomaded pate. Grasping him by the collar she drew him face downward across her knee and rained a shower of resounding whacks upon the area of his white duck trousers most convenient for whacking. Then giving him a two-handed shaking that made his teeth rattle, she flung him back into his seat, his cheeks scarlet, his jaws wide open with amazement.

For a second she stood there, a triumphant Amazon, but aghast at what she had done, dimly realizing she had incurred another penalty for her team. In confusion she laid one hand upon the rail and vaulted down into the court just as the whistle blew for play.

The steel-girdered gymnasium fairly rocked with the explosion of delirious mirth that followed. It lifted the spectators to their feet and did not cease until the bang of the timekeeper's gun brought the game to an end.

Nobody seemed to remember, or care, whether the referee had imposed that penalty or not. Only a handful of fans recovered their composure in time to see Flossie's superb throw that gave the Boomers a two-point victory in the last five seconds of play. Herbie Wilson, they say, didn't think to ask who won the game until the next day.

Preachin' Jake, edging his way out of the gymnasium, came face to face with his daughter as she hurried to the dressing room.

"Gal," he stammered in a voice that was strange even to himself, "yer pappy was plumb proud of ye tonight. But fer the Lord's sake git in thar an' dress. Ye hain't got enough on to wad a shotgun!"

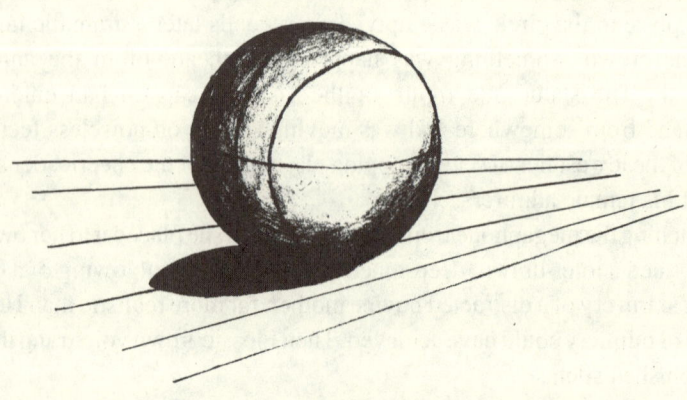

HARMONY CHAPEL

The noisy waters of Big Powderhorn, falling down from the Tennessee side of Thunderhead, cease somewhat their mad tumbling as the narrow gorge widens out into the roomy valley of Galax Cove. Twelve times the creek is crossed by the rocky wagon-road in the five miles of its inhabited course. Four of the crossings are effected by means of crude bridges of unhewn logs. The rest are turbulent fords, easy and safe enough at ordinary season, but difficult or impassable in times of spring freshets or late-winter thaws.

From the lonesome cabin of Huse McKinney, whose heavy pasture-bars close the upper end of the road, down to the little settlement that is the gateway to the wider world of Dry Valley, there are in all about forty homes in Galax. A typical cove of the Southern highlands it is, in that spacious region that runs truer to type than any other section of America—a little hill-locked inlet on the broad stream of Democracy, whose mighty tides send scarce a ripple into its safe seclusion.

You probably wouldn't find Galax Cove on your map of Tennessee. Indeed, old man Jake Howell, who used to be the schoolmaster in the "settle*ment*," declared once that even the name of the place had been "tore out o' the joggafy." Only a faint blue line on the government topographical map, growing imperceptibly heavier as it approaches the broader, bluer band of the Little River, suggests to the imagination the devious path of sparkling rills somersaulting into rivulets that finally unite to form the Big Powderhorn.

But to the folk who live in these forty sequestered homes under the long shadows of Great Smoky, Galax is the very center of the big world whose circumference lies somewhere beyond the blue haze of the environing hills.

Nor is it so circumscribed a world as the outlander is prone to believe. It stretches wide enough for suns to rise and set, for the eternal interplay of day and night, summer and winter, tempest and the calm of placid stars. Wide enough to compass the ultimate metes and bounds of human affairs—birth and death, youth and age, toil and rest, love and hate, hope and despair.

Life in the little-big world of the cove keeps somehow close to things elemental. The grim, bare-handed struggle for physical existence in the half-cleared wilderness occupies body, mind, and heart during most of the short span between belated sunrise and mid-afternoon twilight. For the rest—the soul-cravings that food, raiment, and shelter cannot satisfy—the mind of the cove-dweller is driven inward upon itself, and he becomes introspective, instinctively religious. In such an environment as his, the seeds of asceticism and fatalism in his Calvinistic traditions fall upon fertile soil. His religion becomes a major concern, but is yet a thing apart in the drab routine of his unending grapple with nature.

Time was when the two tiny "church-houses" in Galax Cove, the Hardshell and the Methodist, stood over against each other like two frowning forts bristling with menacing guns.

When "Preacher Ike" Gallaher hobbled down the valley to preach in the Hardshell meeting-house, or perhaps to "hold a babtizin'" in the dark pool at the edge of the churchyard, the old man came with no soft gospel of compromise or tolerance toward the "onscriptural teachin's of these here Methodis' people up the creek." And when Wesley Shelton, the gray-haired circuit-rider from Dry Valley, preached to his smaller flock in the "upper meetin'-house," he came as Elijah came to Carmel, to rout the enemies of Jehovah and lead the prophets of Baal down to the brook and slay them there.

But that was before "the big tide."

It had been a forward spring in the hills. The sunny first days of April had brought "corn-plantin' time" earlier than usual. Far up on the southern slopes the white-canvas squares of tobacco-beds gleamed in the morning light. Nature, defying all the canons of the artist with shocking discords of red and yellow and pink streaked against the gray of sandstone cliff, the brown of plowed hillside or the shifting greens that paled away into the sky-line, achieved a harmony no artist ever dared to copy.

With corn in the ground, tobacco planted, and "sweet-'tater slips" bedded thus early, the farmers in the cove had more than their wonted leisure in the early summer. Preacher Ike, as an ever-watchful laborer in the Lord's vineyard, discerned the signs of the time as auspicious for a "protracted meetin'." Accordingly it was "norated around" that there would be "preachin' ever' night at early candle-lightin', beginnin' with the new of the moon in May."

Picture a little congregation of some sixty folk seated on rough hand-made benches, men on one side, women on the other. On little wooden brackets along the walls, four small, smoky kerosene-lamps alleviate the darkness with a weird half-light.

The gaunt form of Preacher Ike "weaves" rhythmically back and forth as he warms up to the message of the hour. His nasal singsong, punctuated with grotesque "Ahs!" long drawn out, fills the narrow room and pours through the open windows, to be beaten back in echoes from the vertical mountain walls across the valley.

There was something strangely gripping about the rude eloquence of the illiterate parson of Galax Cove. The more sophisticated of the mountain youth had learned to laugh at his primitive delivery, but the more thoughtful sensed the indubitable power of the preacher—something perhaps akin to that which once drew scribe and Pharisee into the wilderness to hear one dressed not in soft raiment or shaken like a reed in the wind, but a prophet and much more than a prophet.

It chanced that the new moon of May fell on the third Sunday. Night after night for two weeks the meeting went on, and the congregations grew with the fervor of the preacher. A few of the Methodist adherents came, partly through the irresistible attraction of a revival upon the mountain mind, partly through a half-concealed truculence, to hear what the preacher "really did say agin the Methodis'."

They came seeking, and they went away having found. Bold with a courage worthy of the noblest cause, the old Hardshell prophet knew naught but to deliver the oracles of Jehovah as he heard them through the thick walls of his cribbed and cabined soul. His mind, untutored, was yet keenly and coldly logical. With his major premise based upon the unshaken word of revelation as interpreted by those of his own creed, and his minor premise supplied by the unbelieving Wesleyans, there could be but one conclusion. The Methodists might be sincere, they might be well-meaning folk, but they deliberately rejected the plain teachings of the Scriptures. Hence they followed a road that in the end must lead to hell.

"I tell ye right now," he shouted, "that God A'mighty didn't never have to save nobody at all—ah! He done it jest of His own free will-ah! An' He laid down in this here book jest how He aimed to do itah! Hit says, 'Repent an' be babtized—ah!' An' then hit goes on an' tells jest *how* to be babtized. Hit don't say nary word about sprinklin' nor pourin'—ah! Hit says John the Babtis' led the Son of Man right down *inter* the water, an' atter he babtized Him, he led Him up *outen* the water."

"I tell ye, people, that they's some around here that preaches what ain't in this here Bible—ah! An' I tell ye they's a-leadin' immortal souls into slippery places. An' as sure as this Good Book's true from kiver to kiver, they's goin' to come a time when ye got to answer the Jedge when he axes ye, 'Why ain't ye got on a weddin'-garment'—ah?' An' then the Jedge is goin' to say: 'Ye hain't done what the Book said. Depart from me—I never knowed ye!'"

As might have been expected, the word went forth and finally came to the ears of Brother Wes Shelton that the walls of Methodism on Big Powderhorn were being sorely beleaguered. It was even rumored that some of Tobe McIntosh's family had "jined up" with the Baptists and that further defections were imminent.

When that call from the Lord's people in distress reached Brother Wes, all that was finest, most heroic in him responded to the clarion voice of duty.

Mounting his old mare, Magalene—so named, he said, because as a filly she had been possessed of seven devils—he rode to the help of Israel.

It was near sundown on Saturday before the fifth Sunday of May when he drew rein at the "uppin' block" in front of Nath Walker's "tub mill." Half a score of the men of the cove were gathered here, waiting each his turn while the tiny mill in its ancient way "first ground one grain and then started on another."

"Howdy, gentlemens?" was Brother Wes's greeting. "How's she grindin'?"

"Purty slow, Brother Shelton; purty slow. The dry spell's run the water powerful low," Nath, the miller, drawled. "Won't ye light and rest yer nag a while?"

"I reckon not," the preacher demurred. "I'll be gittin' along up the creek a ways."

"I 'low ye'll hold meetin' to-morrer in the upper church," ventured Nath. Nath was one of Brother Wes's staunch supporters. His tone was intentionally casual, but the query was designed as an "opener."

"The Lord willin', I aim to do it. I reckon some of you-uns'll be out to the preachin'," replied Brother Wes, turning Magalene's head up the road.

"Reckon ye heared they was a big meetin' a-goin' on in the Babtis' church?" Nath threw out his final challenge to draw the preacher's fire.

"I heared a little about it," Brother Wes retorted, "an' I 'lowed I'd have somethin' to say about it to-morrer."

Old Magalene's iron shoes clinked defiantly upon the "river rocks" as she and her rider disappeared round the sharp turn.

"Fifth Sunday" dawned clear and warm. For weeks the succession of cloudless days and balmy nights had been unbroken. Saturday night the full moon had poured its mild charity upon jagged cliff and bristling spur, softening all their harshness into gentleness. But it was remembered afterward that old Grandad Peterson, smoking his bedtime pipe in his dooryard, had described a "sarcle" round the moon.

The laconic implication of the Reverend Wesley Shelton's farewell remark to the group at the mill did not miss its mark. By the almost uncanny freemasonry of the mountaineers, the word was bruited up and down the length of the cove before nightfall that "Brother Wes was goin' to light into the Babtis' a-Sunday mornin'." Even Huse McKinney at the end of the road tightened the shoes on his dilapidated mule by lantern-light, preparatory to a ride down the valley on the morrow.

Despite the momentum of interest that two weeks of Preacher Ike's vociferations had developed, drawing goodly numbers even from the rival camp, the certainty of a dramatic counter-offensive from the fiery Methodist filled the upper church on the eventful fifth Sunday morning. Not a few even of the Baptist persuasion found the prospect of a theological sword-clash more appealing than the sonorous reiteration of their favorite doctrines. Even Grandad Peterson, the senior deacon in the Hardshell church, doubted if his rheumatic knee was equal to the long walk down to the "big meetin'," and stopped for the first time in his life to worship with the Methodist brethren.

Those who remembered Wesley Shelton as a young man told thrilling tales of his prowess in the arts that constitute the pentathlon of the mountain youth— running, lifting, wrestling, boxing ("knocking") and swimming. Even now his eye had not lost its luster, and his tall frame, though bent with the burdens of seven decades, gave still the suggestion of a power that might be summoned at need.

To-day, though, he seemed more aged and weary than fiery as he sat crosslegged on the bare platform behind the rude desk, although the early comers, as they sat in expectant silence, sensed something ominous in the outward calm of the old warrior.

Long afterward, many of the little congregation used to speak of that "fif'-Sunday meetin'."

"I jest set thar a-thinkin'," Aunt Louviny Whitehead would relate over and over, "of the day he married me an' Ben. I mind it jest like hit was yesterday. I'd allus heared him preachin' in his big roarin' voice, but that day he was plumb gentle, and his voice was soft and easy-like."

"Yes," Tildy Walker, mother of Nath Walker's eleven children, would add; "I was allus kind o' skeered of him till he come an' et at our house. Then I seed how he tuck on over the little uns. He'd take the little setalongs on his knee and talk to 'em when they hadn't never seen no strangers afore, an' they wasn't afeared of him nary bit. An' then when he buried our little Virgie an' I could jest see his eyes a-puddlin', I knowed then Brother Wes was a shore-enough man of God."

Strange mixture indeed he was of gentleness and ferocity, of broad sympathy and bitter prejudice, of compassion for sinners and implacable hatred of heretics. To-day, though, the iron was deep in his soul. The Church of his fathers, the faith once committed to the saints, had been attacked. Some of the little flock whom he had sought to lead in green pastures had been enticed into strange by-paths, and were all but ready to turn their backs upon what was to him the very fold of truth itself.

"Brethren, my tex' to-day is from the old Book of Genesis: 'An' God said unto Noey, the end of all flesh is come before me; for the earth is filled with violence. An' behold I do bring the flood of waters upon the earth to destroy all flesh.'"

"When I seed him a-thumbin' in the fore part of the Good Book," Huse McKinney reported to his wife, Cordie, on his return, "I knowed he was a huntin' a tex' to skeer the ungodly with. An' he shore done it. He cert'nly showed 'em up, too," Huse continued. "These here deep-water Babtists a-puttin' their trust in goin' under the water instid o' gittin' under the blood! Why, Cordie, hit was plumb fearsome the way he showed 'em the wrath of God a-comin' like the flood in the days of Noey!"

"I kin hear him yit a-sayin': 'O my hearers, I tell ye the floods of waters is a-comin'. Some of you-uns has been tryin' to put yer trust in the waters o' Powderhorn, like as if *hit* could save yer guilty souls! O sinner, I tell ye the floods o' God's wrath is a-comin' down Powderhorn, an' they's a-comin' soon!'"

It was a sober little throng that filed out of the weather-beaten church after the sermon. As the people stood round the churchyard in little groups, unhitching their horses or seating the children in the straw-filled wagon-beds for the homeward journey, there was much comment on the sermon.

Among the Methodists, naturally, there was much nodding of approving heads and an unconcealed elation over the evident discomfiture of the Baptists present. Grandad Peterson gripped his old walking-stick tightly as he limped up the dusty road, but his only comment was:

Courtesy of the Great Smoky Mountains National Park   Photographed by Edouard E. Exline

The Jim Carr Tub Mill worked on the Little Pigeon River until it was destroyed by a flood in 1951.

"Well, I 'low the Lord A'mighty knows more about who'll git drownded when the floods comes than some that holds theirselves up fer prophets."

And Grandad's stick rapped smartly on the stones as he turned toward his cottage nestling on a "bench" of the mountain, a hundred yards above the road.

When he had climbed the steep path up to his little yard, he turned a moment to take in the familiar view down the narrow valley. As his aged eyes rested upon the quieting harmony of landscape and skyline, his weather-wise glance did not fail to note the scalloped crest of a summer cloud showing just above the dim outline of far-away Clingmans Dome. As he turned and lifted the latch of his cabin door, he thought he heard the distant rumble of thunder.

Preacher Ike, after a sermon filled with denunciations the more scathing because of the diminished congregation of the "fifth Sunday," was walking up the road to take dinner at the home of his son Lincoln, whose steep orchard rose sharply from the back yard of his cabin on the creek. Just before he reached the foot-log that led from the road across to Link Gallaher's house, he heard a horse's hoofs on the rocks and, looking up, saw Brother Wes swaying from side to side on his faithful Magalene.

It was the first time for many months that the two men had been face to face. With the echoes of their respective philippics still in their ears, each was obviously nonplused for a word of recognition to exchange with his antagonist. The stinging sense of having suffered reproach for righteousness' sake could not be ignored.

And thus the two prophets of the Lord, meeting in the way, passed on. No word was spoken, but in the look that each gave the other was fanatical, implacable hate. It was just at this moment that Grandad Peterson thought he heard the distant rumble of thunder.

In a land where newspapers seldom come and where weather-bulletins and barometers are either unknown or held in less repute than the local weather-prophet and the almanac, people must take the weather day by day as it comes. The folk in Galax knew nothing of the storm-warnings that had gone forth into every city and hamlet where the newspaper goes. They knew nothing and cared nothing about the unusual cyclonic disturbances in the Caribbean which had been moving landward for days.

They knew only that across Thunderhead that Sunday evening there swept one of the spectacular summer storms that have given the peak its name. From the dooryards and rude porticoes they could hear the premonitory rumblings from the black cloud rolling in terrific grandeur over the giant rampart from Thunderhead to the Miry Ridge.

Then the storm swept down the great transverse ridges of the Tennessee highlands, filling the ravines and deep hollows with indescribable tumult.

Tumult of shrieking winds, of snapping branches and up-rooted trunks thrown crisscross on the mountainsides. Tumult of crashing, appalling thunder-din, caught up and hurled back from a hundred cliffs and crags. And through it all the swish of blinding sheets of rain, swelling crystal rills into mad torrents and frothy cascades.

The storm passed quickly, but all night the lightning signaled back and forth from Thunderhead to far-away LeConte. Toward morning the main body of the cloud masses driven by cyclonic winds began to drop their burdens of moisture as they rose to the upper levels of the mountain barrier. All day it rained, not the gentle rain of a summer day but the downpour of a tropical storm. At nightfall of Monday, Tobe McIntosh "lowed the clouds looked thinner," but Grandad Peterson shook his sage old head.

"I've been a-settin' an' a-readin' the almanac to-day, an' the signs is right fer a heap of fallin' weather. Somehow, I can't git it out o' my head what that thar preacher man said a-Sunday about the floods a-comin'."

Once more Grandad was vindicated of his prophecies. Monday night and Tuesday, Tuesday night and Wednesday, the rain never ceased. Wednesday night, many thought the rain grew heavier than ever. Thursday dawned dark and cold, but the rain fell unabated.

On Monday afternoon, Nath Walker, the miller, was able to handle the grists as they came, for the night's storm had raised the low waters to their normal stage. Tuesday, the little flume that supplied the primitive horizontal wheel was spilling the yellow water over the mill-timbers. At noon Wednesday, Nath abandoned the mill, as the flood threatened to cut off the approach from the road in front. Late that evening, the mill went out.

With foot-logs all washed away and the fords impassable, Galax Cove was cut in two, with no possible means of communication across the dividing stream. Even the booming voice of big Davy Holder gave up the futile attempt to shout a warning across to Link Gallaher that the water was stealthily creeping round his house. Link, standing on his porch, tried hard to catch big Davy's excited voice and gesticulations, but the deafening roar drowned both sound and sense.

Preacher Ike sat in the doorway, holding on his knee his favorite grandchild, little Beulah, Link's five-year-old "baby." The little one was looking with big-eyed wonder at the yellow flood rolling past the front gate, and clinging in half-terror round her grandfather's neck.

"Grandaddy," she whimpered, "what did Dod let hit come so much big water fer? Did ole Wes Shelton ax Him to, like Grandad Peterson said he done?"

"Why, child, whatever put sech a idee in your leetle head? Wes Shelton hain't got no more to do with hit than me or yer paw," the old man replied. But his heart was less calm than his words.

"Never mind, honey; jest you trust in the Lord an' hit'll be all right," he added comfortingly. And the little maid's heart grew stouter at his words.

Nobody in Galax slept that Wednesday night. Before bedtime a disturbing rumor went up and down the line of watchers on the north bank that Ferd Davenport's house had been undermined and was adrift; but the report could not be confirmed, as Ferd lived on "yan side."

All night the thunder of the relentless storm overhead was drowned entirely by the more terrible thunder of the waters. The narrow creek-bed was washed into a broad river-channel, down which the drift scudded—countless logs, occasional bridges, haycocks, hen-coops and small outbuildings. From the depths of the channel came the horrible grinding of rocks, titanic boulders rolling and sliding upon the primordial floor of the gorge. Small islands went by, with trees still standing erect, sometimes with frightened fowls aroost in their branches.

Big Davy's warning could not have saved the Gallaher house even if it could have been understood. When the first dim light of morning came, Link realized that the house and barn were hopelessly cut off. Tearing off the heavy battened door of the log kitchen, he tried, with the help of his wife and Preacher Ike, to construct a raft on which the mother and child might reach the higher ground in the rear, where the orchard tilted up the mountainside. The current in the forty-foot space between the back door and the orchard fence was not swift, and Link hoped he could get the little family to safety by pushing the raft across the narrow sluice. Carefully he seated his wife, Cely, with little Beulah in her arms, while he and the grandfather, half wading and half swimming in the shoulder-deep water, pushed the unsteady craft toward the orchard gate.

Just what happened the next moment no one could ever tell. All that Link or his father can recall is that the four of them were suddenly struggling in the deep water and drifting down toward where the backyard sluice rejoined the main current. Somehow, Link got hold of Cely and fought his way to the roots of a big chestnut at the edge of the orchard. From there they saw the frantic struggle of the aged father to reach the escaping raft, to the edge of which the child was clinging with the desperation of one drowning. But the strength of the grandfather's reckless lunges was puny when matched against the might of the torrent, and his yearning fingers missed the baby's floating garments by a hand-breadth.

It was all that Link and Cely could do to restrain the old man from his insane impulse to plunge down the current in the wake of the raft and its ill-fated little passenger. When they had finally dragged him to the roots of the chestnut where they had found footing, he threw himself forward with a mighty cry that was mostly a prayer:

"O God A'mighty, God A'mighty—my leetle Beulah gal! Ye can save her, God, and nobody else can't! Send a angel and save her, or else take me with her!"

"Git up, paw, an' help Link!" Cely was shouting with the preternatural calm that mothers have when stout-hearted men go to pieces in whimpering supplications. "He's tryin' to git holt of that thar door with a pole. We've got to save my baby, and do hit quick!"

Cely was running now down the bank, watching the raft and the clinging child as the current tossed them about like specks of foam. It was broad daylight now, and through the swaying willows the excited watchers on the other side had just become alive to the tragedy that was being enacted across the creek. A dozen men and boys were running along the farther bank, keeping pace with the raft and with the frantic parents and grandfather on the nearer side.

Suddenly a tall figure dashed through the crowd of running men and plunged headlong into the flood. Nobody had time to see or ask who it was. They saw only that a head, half hidden under a broad-brimmed felt hat, was bobbing up and down on the crest of the boiling tide and was being propelled by long, powerful strokes farther and farther into midstream and keeping abreast of the tossing raft. There were strong swimmers among the mountain youth, but in a flood like this no sane man would even hope to cross the current.

Courtesy of the Great Smoky Mountains National Park   Photographed by Charles S. Grossman
Cades Cove Methodist Episcopal Church - 1937.

But the head under the old felt hat kept atop of the seething swirls and was visibly gaining on the raft. Preacher Ike saw the unknown swimmer gradually closing the distance between himself and the frail bark that held the little life the old man loved better than his own.

"Look out thar, Link!" he shouted hoarsely, as he stumbled on. "God A'mighty has sent a angel to save leetle Beulah! Glory! Glory! Glory!"

And the angel of the Lord did save little Beulah. With one final burst of almost superhuman strength, the tall swimmer clutched the edge of the old kitchen door, and with his other arm caught the body of the little girl just as her own tiny fingers were relaxing their clasp on the thick boards. The rescuer then guided the raft toward a projecting ledge of rock that marked a sharp bend in the creek. Upon this ledge Link Gallaher had leaped, in the hope of reaching the raft with his pole.

As the door struck the rock, little Beulah was thrown forward by the sharp impact right into the outstretched arms of her father, whose shout of joy could be heard even across the stream. But the raft and the swimmer were whirled round the ledge and into the mad stream again. There was no strength left, though, in the long arms that had been so mighty to save. The helpless watchers on both banks saw the tense fingers slip inch by inch from their precarious hold on the slippery door. But in that moment of final, hopeless struggle, the swimmer's face was turned upward for a moment, so that all could see.

"Hit's Brother Wes, and he's a-drownin' right afore our eyes!" shouted big Davy.

They found Wesley Shelton's body three days later, lodged in a huge pile of drift two miles down the creek. In a rude coffin of hand-ripped walnut boards, the broken body was hauled back the long, hard drive over flood-washed roads to the little Methodist meeting-house behind which lay the old burying-ground. It would be weeks yet before the roads to Dry Valley could be traveled or a preacher of Brother Wes's own faith could come into Galax.

With one accord, therefore, the mountain folk, including the widowed sister of Brother Wes, Aunt Rachel McTavish, turned to Preacher Ike. They still say in Galax: "The biggest buryin' that was ever seed in this settle*ment* was Brother Wes Shelton's atter the big tide. An' nobody hain't never heared sich a preachin' as Preacher Ike give that day."

The Sunday-afternoon sun, slanting through the windows of the little church, fell upon the stolid faces of the assembled friends and upon the rude bier supported upon two splint-bottomed chairs in front of the pulpit. The silence was broken only by an occasional scraping of a heavy boot on the floor or by a subdued moan from Aunt Rachel. Behind the bier, on the low platform, Preacher Ike rose slowly and stepped forward on the creaking boards.

"Friends and neighbors," he began, "you-uns all know what has brung us out here to-day. I never 'lowed I'd ever be a-standin' in this meetin'-house a-tryin' to say somethin' about the man that used to preach to you here. Him an' me was travelin' fur apart on our road to the Better Land. I were on one side of the water an' he were on the other. You-uns has heared me say some mighty hard things about him an' his teachin's. God A'mighty knows I was tryin' the best I knowed how to preach what I larnt outen his Good Book."

"But las' Thursday mornin' the good Lord sent one of His angels down here to save my leetle Beulah out o' the turrible flood of waters. I seed that angel splunge right into the tide an' swim like no man on earth ever swum afore, till he throwed my baby sqar' into her daddy's arms. An' when they told me that thar angel was my feller man an' brother, Wes Shelton, before God, people, hit plumb tore my ole heart outen my bosom."

"I ain't worthy nor fitten to be standin' here over this coffin, but I tell ye, if ever the good Lord opens them pearly gates fer me—an' I hope hit won't be long now—I'm a-goin' to ax fust fer one leetle peep at the blessed Savior, an' then jest a teeny word with my own Marthy that's been a-waitin' thar fer me twenty year. An' then I'm a-goin' to hunt up an' down them streets till I find Wes Shelton, an' I'll git him by the hand an' ax him to take an' interduce me to God A'mighty."

The little Hardshell chapel had been swept away along with Nath Walker's mill and half a score other buildings in the cove. It has never been rebuilt. But the upper church has been remodeled. The mountain folk call it "Sweet Harmony Chapel," and they say it's the only meeting-house in the Smokies that has both a Methodist chancel before the altar and a baptismal font beside the pulpit steps.

FOREWORD TO TALL TALES FROM OLD SMOKY 1952

It seemed appropriate to include these words of Hodge Mathes' wife, Wynema Souder Mathes, which introduced the first printing of a collection of Hodge Mathes' work. Tall Tales From Old Smoky *contained most of the stories in this book. Wynema Mathes' words are helpful in understanding a little more of the author, her husband.*

About forty-five years ago, Charles Hodge Mathes was Professor of Greek at Maryville College in Tennessee. The lofty peaks of the Great Smoky Mountains, so near at hand, had an irresistible appeal. The writer and his colleagues spent many holidays and vacations exploring them.

Not only had the untamed wilderness a glorious appeal to the author, but the PEOPLE who lived there in sturdy, independent isolation. These were the hardy souls of English and Scotch-Irish stock whose ancestors had pushed on from the coast to the tall, aloof mountains and found there the peace and freedom they sought. Positive traces of the Elizabethan speech delighted Hodge Mathes. His fine linguistic mind found rhythm and poetry there. The people he met in the mountains became his friends ... as did those he met in the cities. His sensitive understanding, his genuine love of his fellow men, and his gentleness were his outstanding traits.

So Hodge Mathes wrote of the mountain people in his beloved Southern Appalachians. He wrote of their loves, their hates, their adventures, and their problems, all with a clear concept of the world in which they lived. These people, this section of America, no longer exist as they did in those days.

In 1911 Hodge Mathes went to what is now East Tennessee State College as Academic Dean. During the next forty years he continued to visit and write about the mountains. He lived to see the opening up of the heretofore inaccessible regions ... by the mission schools, the roads and railroads. He lived to see the mountain cabin give way to a modern dwelling; the cook fireplace bow to the electric stove powered by TVA. He lived to see the sons, daughters and grandchildren of his mountain friends graduate from fine colleges and take their places in a larger society.

You won't meet the people of whom he wrote anymore ... not even on the Maine to Georgia trail across the mountain tops, which the author helped to break. You can make your camp on Mount LeConte or The Grandfather and be visited by an uninvited bear. Should you wander too far off the trail in some sections, you might even come upon "moonshiners." But they are a new people ... not the stalwart pioneer whose dignity and character so impressed Hodge Mathes.

The stories contained in this book were previously published by current magazines. This volume has been printed as a memorial to my husband, Hodge Mathes, and to an American Era, which, like the author, has passed away.

                                        Wynema Souder Mathes
                                        April, 1952

The stories of C. Hodge Mathes have previously been published in magazines and books. A collection of Hodge Mathes' stories, under the title <u>Tall Tales of Old Smoky</u>, was published by Wynema Souder Mathes, Hodge Mathes' wife, in 1952. The stories were also published as follows:

    A Saga of the Carolina Hills - <u>The High Road</u>, 1929
    The Linkster - <u>Everybody's First in Fiction</u>, 1924
    The Draggin'est Feller - <u>Everybody's First in Fiction</u>, 1924
    Simple Ike's Daughter - <u>Extension Magazine</u>, 1937
    Jeff Howell's Buryin' - <u>Tennessee Folklore Society Bulletin</u>, 1940
    White Mule - <u>Munsey's</u>, 1929
    The Curin'est Remedy - <u>Popular Magazine</u>, 1929
    "Vengeance Is Mine!" - <u>Young People's Weekly</u>, 1928
    For The High Dollar - <u>Blade and Ledger</u>, 1930
    What Is To Be Will Be - <u>The Southern Planter</u>, 1929
    Corpus Delicti - <u>Extension Magazine</u>, 1936
    Willow Pattern - <u>Extension Magazine</u>, 1937
    Shake Rag Shows 'Em - <u>The Farmer's Wife</u>, 1933
    Harmony Chapel - <u>Everybody's First in Fiction</u>, 1923

Also available from *Panther Press*

As a companion to this book, "In the Shadow of Old Smoky" on audio tape is also available. This sixty minute tape contains four stories from the book, told by storyteller Charles Maynard.

WATERFALLS AND CASCADES OF THE GREAT SMOKY MOUNTAINS

"The Smokies were and are carved by water. Water has shaped the mountains and valleys into their present form. Stand on a peak to look down on the jumble of mountains ridges, valleys and ravines. Look carefully. Notice the slopes, the peaks, the twinkle of sunlight on water. Water sculpted this marvelous landscape."

Waterfalls and Cascades is a guidebook to over thirty waterfalls and cascades in the Great Smoky Mountains National Park. Twenty-eight color and black and white photographs illustrate this volume which locate the falls with maps and text. History, both natural and human, is revealed through the writing of Hal Hubbs, Charles Maynard, and David Morris. Enjoy the magic of the mountains as it is experienced at waterfalls with this book.

TIME WELL SPENT FAMILY HIKING IN THE SMOKIES

"Family hiking doesn't have to be a frustrating struggle, but it does involve more than just walking a mountain trail. The key to enjoyment is planning ahead." *Time Well Spent* assists families in planning for walks in the Smokies with 35 enjoyable hikes for all types of families, 7 maps with good directions to all areas of the national park, 15 short nature and historical trails which reveal life in the Smokies then and now, suggestions for finding waterfalls, fire towers, historic buildings, wildflowers, virgin forest and scenic views. Included are interesting stories and legends about the region and a handy index for quick reference.

To order books or tapes write **Panther Press, P.O. Box 636, Seymour, TN 37865**. Include $1 shipping per item ordered.

Title	Price per copy	Quantity	Total
Waterfalls & Cascades	$7.95		
Time Well Spent	$6.95		
In The Shadow of Old Smoky	$8.95		
AudioTape- In The Shadow of Old Smoky	$8.95		
		Shipping/handling	
		Total Enclosed	